Working Out WEST

CHAPTER ONE
WEST

Death was at my door when I opened it. Not figuratively, but literally—Death, the person who did security for the place where I worked. He leaned against the wall opposite my room.

"You ready, kid?"

With a shaky smile, I shrugged to play off how I was about to shit myself. "As long as you don't call me kid, sure." I stepped out of my assigned room and into the hall. He started down the hall, and I fell into step beside him. I pressed a hand to my stomach. There was a chance I would vomit, which wouldn't be pretty, so I swallowed thickly and prayed my light dinner wouldn't revolt on me.

"Can't help it. You're a lot younger than me," he said. Then, in the next breath, he gave me the rundown on the device I had to wear on my suit while assuring me he would be my backup for that night.

Were they expecting something to go wrong?

That didn't help my nerves one bit.

In fact, I wondered if Death would mind a pit stop to a toilet, so I didn't shit myself.

"Wait," I said, holding my hand up. Turning, I pressed that palm onto the underground garage wall and breathed deeply to try and control my bodily functions.

I hadn't been kidding. My gut swirled so much it put pressure on my bowels. I inhaled and squeezed my ass cheeks together. If my parents saw me now, they'd disown me. Actually, if my religious and very strict parents saw me and knew I was gay, they'd kick my ass and then disown me. Luckily, they knew nothing about my new job as an escort or the fact I was gay. Something I hid since they would be disgusted.

"West, you okay?"

"Yep," I chirped and used my free hand to give him the thumbs-up.

Death snorted. "You look like you're gonna hurl. You don't have to do this, you know?" His hand landed on my shoulder and gave it a squeeze.

I pressed a palm to my stomach and straightened. *Come on, West. You're being a chicken-shit. You don't even have to have sex. It's a date, for God's sake.*

Nodding to myself, I faced Death, and his hand fell away. "I'm fine. You just threw me with all the protectiveness." I let out a huff of laughter. "Like you think something will go on."

Death smiled softly. Even if he was a large man covered in tats and looked scary, he was still a sweetheart under it all. Not that I would tell him. I'd get my head bitten off.

"Don't stress, kid—fuck, West. I'm sure nothin' will happen."

Nodding again, I sucked in a breath and straightened my suit jacket. "Right. I can do this."

"Yeah, you can, and I'll have your back the entire time."

"That's good to know."

"Besides, if I didn't, Wreck would kick my ass because Lucas would have a word with him for getting his friend into shit."

Laughing, I bobbed my head. "That is true."

Feeling better, I made it the rest of the way to the car Death pointed out. Once there, he handed me the keys. "Drive safe. I'll be right behind you."

"Got it. Thanks."

He tipped his chin up at me in response. Something I noticed a lot of the bikers did. Death was also a part of the Diamond MC. I met the club through Lucas, my friend from college, whose brother was in the club.

They were a good group of people, and if it hadn't been for knowing Lucas, I wouldn't have met them. I probably would have been too scared to, since a lot of them looked like they could kill with one hand tied behind their backs.

Slipping into the car, I put the key in the ignition and started the engine. After another big breath, I put it in Drive and headed out of the underground garage and onto the road. I'd already memorized the address I needed to go to where Mr. Adrik Hail would be waiting for me. My date.

The drive took me half an hour, which was annoying because it gave me more time to fret over this. I parked out on the street to this huge condo complex and quickly got out of the car so I didn't second-guess my choice. My knees were weak, my hands shook, but I sucked in a lungful of air and reminded myself I needed this money.

At least I wasn't selling my body for money, just my time.

You're a sinner. Pray to God for forgiveness. Pray to God.

Words my parents used to say when I got into trouble for something flashed through my mind. No, they could never find out about this. Never.

It would be just another sin added to my life, like wanting to move away from them, even when it wasn't far. It had only been recently they'd started speaking to me again, and only after I'd told them I'd prayed every morning and night for forgiveness.

They were different. I knew this. They were strict, and God was everything to them. My stomach pivoted downward.

Gosh darn it all. Now definitely wasn't the time to think of them. I was doing this for me, to help my future, to set me up, because there wasn't a chance I would go back to living under their roof.

I had to get my head in the game, so I pasted on a smile as I opened the front doors to the building where Mr. Hail lived on the top floor.

Two men stood behind a desk, and both looked up when I entered. Their grave expressions had my smile slipping a little, but I pushed it back up.

Was having men guarding the door a normal thing for condos? I'd heard of doormen before, but these two looked nothing like doormen. Besides the fact they hadn't opened the door for me, they both wore plain black T-shirts, and if I had to guess, since I couldn't see below their waists, they'd have jeans on as well.

One picked up a phone and said something into it in a quiet tone.

"Ben Gowan?" the other man called with a slight accent.

I nodded and walked the rest of the way to the desk. "Yes, I'm me. I mean him…. I'm Ben." *Shit, get it together, man.* The new name, my escort name, had me fumbling like a fool. I had to remember my name so I didn't give anyone my real one.

"Mr. Hail is waiting for you. I'll escort you up."

Wait, what? Why?

"Um, sure, okay." I stepped back and waited for him to move around the desk. He grabbed a jacket on the way. When he walked by, putting on the jacket, my eyes widened when I caught sight of the gun strapped to his back.

Who was this guy? No, more importantly, who was Mr. Hail? A condo didn't need this type of security, did it? For a moment, my hand itched to touch the pin I wore on my suit. This whole scene had me on edge.

At the elevators, the man pressed the button and then turned to me. "Do you mind if I pat you down?"

"Sorry?" I choked.

"Pat you down for weapons," he said seriously and with an intense gaze.

Laughing uncomfortably, I waited for him to join in, thinking he was pulling my leg, but he didn't.

My laughter evaporated. "Right, okay, sure." I nodded. His hands ran over my body quickly, and I found it strange he was doing it now and not when I first walked in. I could have had a gun and shot them both already, then got in the elevator and headed up to kill Mr. Hail. I wasn't sure if mentioning the flaw in their system or not would be good. It could get me killed. Then again, there was a possibility I looked innocent enough they didn't think they needed to check me over until now. Or their skills were that good, and I didn't seem like a threat, but they'd better do their job.

The guy straightened. He nodded just as the doors dinged open. We stepped in, and there was a moment I felt like making conversation to fill the silence, but I didn't know what to say and worried anything I said would sound stupid.

Did he know what I was there for?

Did he know Mr. Hail paid for my company?

Shaking my head slightly, I pushed all thoughts out because none of it mattered. Nothing mattered except getting my head in the game. I wasn't sure my mind would ever really be in the game, though, not at the moment anyway, not since it was my first night. My first client.

My heart galloped in my chest when the doors dinged open. The guard stepped out first. I followed and waited behind him, since he stopped just outside the elevator doors.

A sudden urge to pee filled me when I heard heavy foot-falls on the polished wooden floors.

Then he was there. I peeked over the guard's shoulder when the guard dipped his chin, saying, "Mr. Hail."

"Ostav' nas," Mr. Hail barked.

Oh boy, he had a thick accent. A Russian accent that shot a tingle to my balls.

That wasn't good.

It wasn't good at all.

The guard didn't say anything back to whatever Mr. Hail said. Instead, he turned and jolted slightly when he saw I was behind him. He nodded at me and stepped back into the elevator, pressing the button to close the doors.

I'd turned to watch the guard and realized it would have been better to keep an eye on Mr. Hail. If I had, I wouldn't have been shitting bricks to have to face him. However, I couldn't stay looking at the doors forever. It started to get to the point of awkwardness.

Sucking in a breath, I slowly moved back to where Mr. Hail still stood. His arms were crossed over his broad chest now. A chest that was covered in something I didn't expect. He wasn't in a suit. No, he dressed casually in jeans, boots, and a T-shirt with what looked like some band's logo splashed over the front of it.

I really felt overdressed and uncomfortable.

"You wore suit." His accent rolled through me and lit up my nerves. I'd always been a sucker for accents.

I swallowed, looked down at myself, nodded before lifting my gaze back up, and up some more, since he was taller, before nodding again. The whole time I gave myself a pep talk: I had to harden myself against his voice. "Yes," I said softly.

He grunted. "Come," he ordered before spinning around and stalking off.

He scared me, aroused me, and intrigued me—all within a matter of moments since I'd seen him.

I took a step his way and then back again.

Shit, shit, shit.

I wanted to run, but I couldn't. Clenching my fists at my sides, I walked around the corner, which opened into a large, pristine living room. Only, Mr. Hail wasn't there. Thankfully, I heard clattering coming over from the left side of the room where another doorway stood. I made my way over with my stomach threatening to throw up the minimal food it had in there.

The doorway was a hallway. I started down it until I found another opening, which led me into a chef's dream kitchen. Mr. Hail was at a counter, placing plates down.

"Dinner," he clipped. His accent sent a shiver down my spine.

He wanted me to eat dinner with him? Did he realize how late it was?

Stepping in, I walked over and stopped on the other side of the counter. I wiped my sweaty hands on my pants before holding on to the edge of the counter. "Um, do you need help with anything?"

His gaze rose slowly and locked on to mine. I gulped as he studied me. Hoo-boy, the room seemed to heat even more, and all on its own, because he certainly hadn't moved to turn up the thermostat.

"Yes? No?" Crap, did he understand what I was saying? He spoke a few words in English, but maybe he preferred Russian? Had Saint or one of the other bosses messed up and sent the wrong person for Mr. Hail? "Sorry, I don't know Russian. You probably prefer to speak that, and I'm unable to, but I promise I can try to understand if you still want to have dinner with me. I'm good at charades. We could act out what we want to say if you can't understand me."

Charades? Seriously, why did I fucking say that? I could have nut-punched myself.

He turned to the stove. "Russian is my first language, but I understand English."

A blush hit my cheeks. Now I felt like a complete moron.

"Right, of course. Sorry for thinking otherwise." I stared down at the counter and ran my fingers over the cool marble. "So," I drew out. "Did you want a hand with something? I'm not a good cook, but I can cut, boil, bake treats, and plate up like a pro." I blanched. My eyes widened, and I looked up to see him watching me. "Not a pro as in prostitute, but a professional. I meant professional."

His stern gaze softened for a second, not even that, maybe a fraction of a second before he said, "Go. Sit." He nodded behind me, and I looked over my shoulder to find a table, which was already set.

"Right." I nodded. God, he probably wanted to eat already so he could get me out of there. I was an idiot to think I could act cool and aloof with clients when deep down, I was still a bumbling idiot. I quickly moved over to the table and sat. I wasn't foolish enough to sit at the head of the table. Mr. Hail certainly looked like he was in charge, and his position was set in stone. Even with the small amount of time I'd spent in the building, I could see the man wasn't one to be messed with.

It had me wondering why he needed company from an

escort in the first place. Why didn't he just have one of his friends over for dinner and a chat?

Whatever it was, it wasn't my place to question his motives. I was there to do a job, and if Mr. Hail wanted to eat dinner with me, we would. Besides, it smelled amazing.

I jolted when a bowl was placed in front of me. I glanced down, and my mouth watered.

"Beef stroganoff," Mr. Hail stated as he put his own bowl down and sat.

I smiled. I didn't let it wither when he just stared at me, giving me nothing. Instead, I said, "Thank you. It looks and smells amazing." I picked up my fork and took a mouthful, moaning as the taste exploded in my mouth. I opened my eyes, which I hadn't realized I'd closed, to see Mr. Hail had been watching me still. He didn't pick up his fork until I nodded and mumbled, "It's great."

He grunted and started eating. Silence rent the room except for our forks and the slight sound of munching. I really didn't do well when things got quiet. In fact, I got more nervous. I felt like I needed to speak and make things comfortable, but I was fighting myself, unsure Mr. Hail was looking for someone to start dribbling shit about nothing in general.

So, I would sit there in silence.

I could.

I had to, because he certainly wasn't saying anything.

Silence was good.

Oh, look over there to the row of floor-to-ceiling windows that I can jump out. I just have to move the transparent curtains. Why do people get see-through curtains? Wait, it looks like there's a balcony. At least I won't have to climb out a window.

Yep, silence was so much fun.

Well, what do we have here? There's a dead plant sitting in a pot at the end of the row of windows. Maybe the silence killed it.

On my last forkful, the silence got to me, and when I placed the fork down in the bowl, I rambled, "My mom cooked beef stroganoff once, but it was nothing like this. She also couldn't say the words as well as you do." Heat hit my cheeks, and I quickly went on. "But when Dad complained about the meat being too tough, she never tried again and stuck to her normal meals she was used to cooking. They mainly contained sausage and vegetables. Meatloaf and vegetables. Lamb stews and chicken and rice. There were other plain dishes, but nothing to rave about. It wasn't until I reached high school and was allowed to attend my first and only sleepover that I discovered pizza." I groaned. "I never knew love until I had my first taste."

Laughing, I shook my head. I hadn't once looked at him while I spoke; instead, I gazed out the windows or down at the table. "When I started college and moved out, I kind of went crazy with all types of takeout, but I soon realized it wasn't good for my bank account. Still, I spoil myself once a week with it." Where the hell was I going with this conversation? "Anyway," I drew out, sliding my fork back and forth in the bowl. "Do you eat takeout?" Did that sound rude? Did it sound like I didn't enjoy the meal? Shit, I was getting paid to be here, and now it sounded like I was judging his food or the fact he cooked by mentioning takeout. With wide eyes, I dragged them up and spewed the words, "Wait, I didn't mean I didn't like dinner. I did, and I appreciate you cooking. I wish I could cook. Seriously, that was the best meal I've had in a long time because I'm not a good cook."

"I know you liked it," Mr. Hail replied, and that was it.

I slumped as the tension rolled off me. "Well, that's good then." I smiled. What did we do now? Did he want to watch a movie? Read a book together? Did I suggest something? If I didn't look away from his lips, he would get an idea I liked them. I didn't. His full, pink lips weren't spank-worthy material. I pulled my gaze up to his dark blue eyes that matched well with his dark blond hair. The sides were shaved close to the scalp, but on top was party time with a messy length that sat over to the left side of his face.

If I weren't gay, I was sure the sight of Mr. Hail could turn me.

Clearing my throat, I glanced away. "Um, this is a nice place you have. Do you work from here?"

"Nyet."

I knew that word meant no. I'd heard it on some movie. He wasn't very forthcoming, but then again, I wasn't here for him to open up to. I felt myself burning up, knowing he was looking at me, yet I didn't want to meet his intense gaze. Instead, I stood slowly, moving my chair back. "I'll take these to the sink." I smiled. "You cooked. The least I can do is clean." Before he could protest, I quickly took his bowl and walked around the counter. I started rinsing the bowls and pan when I noticed Mr. Hail standing opposite me, watching.

"At least you have a dishwasher," I said, opening said

machine to pile the things in. "I don't have one in the unit I live in. I wash everything by hand. Not that I mind, it gives me time to think and go over things I'd learned in college that day."

"What you study?"

Gosh, I loved his accent. "What" sounded like it started with a *v* instead of a *w*. But shit, I wasn't sure if I was supposed to talk about myself—my real life—or make something up. If I did make one up, would I remember what I told him if I came back?

Stuff it. I had to go with the truth. He knew me as Ben anyway, so it wasn't like he could look me up. "I'm studying medicine. I'm training to be a doctor." His reply was to hum under his breath. Of course I went on. "It's hard, but I know it'll be worth it in the end."

I picked up a sponge and wiped down the counter. I placed the sponge on the edge of the sink and grinned over at Mr. Hail. "All clean." What did we do now? I wanted to ask, but I planned to keep my lips sealed this time to see if Mr. Hail said anything.

And he did. "You play chess?"

"I do, Mr. Hail. I'm a master at it, so be ready for me to kick your butt."

His lips twitched. "We will see." He turned and ordered over his shoulder. "Come."

I followed him into the living room, where a chess set sat on the coffee table in the middle of the room. Mr. Hail sat on the couch, and I moved around to the other side. I took off my jacket, placed it on the sofa behind me, and rolled up my sleeves before sitting on the floor instead of the couch. There was just enough room for me. Mr. Hail watched me, something he seemed to like to do. I glanced away and took in the massive television mounted on the wall to my left. Then the bookcases on either side of the screen. There were many books, and I had an urge to see what the man read but didn't.

"Ready?" I asked, looking up at him.

He grunted with a nod.

"You can make the first move, Mr. Hail." I turned the board around so the white side faced him.

"Adrik," he commanded as he reached out and took the first move.

My heart skipped a beat. "Adrik," I whispered with a nod. "And I'm Ben," I told him, which he probably already knew. Yet, I found myself wishing I could have used my real name with him. Oh, fuck me. This man had me twisted inside. I had to keep reminding myself he was a client, because I had a feeling it would be easy for me to like him, even when he was standoffish.

CHAPTER TWO
WEST

*O*nce again, my stomach acted up as I rode the elevator to Mr. Hail's condo. *Sorry, Adrik.* I had to remember he wanted me to call him Adrik, since he'd reminded me many times last time as we played chess. A game, to his shock from the quick flash of wide eyes, I'd won. But of course, he didn't let the shock show long. All he did was look at me and nod.

This time around, I was alone. His security stayed on the main floor and hadn't even patted me down before I got on the elevator with my basket of baked goods.

I wasn't sure why I felt the need to make some muffins for Adrik, but I just did it when the thought dropped into my mind. Now I felt like I was Little Red Riding Hood heading into the woods where I knew the wolf would be waiting.

I'd been surprised when Country had told me Adrik had booked me in for every second weekend. Shocked, but also pleased. It meant I didn't fuck up. It meant he didn't mind my rambling. It also meant he liked my company. Knowing that blasted my stomach with those swirly flying bugs that I couldn't think of the name of. My mind and eyes were too focused on the doors right in front of me as a ding sounded before they slid open slowly.

I expected Adrik to be waiting, but he wasn't. Then I heard sounds coming from the kitchen, so I made my way through his house and called, "Adrik?"

"*Da*, kitchen," he said gruffly back. A shiver ran over my body at his voice, and my dick gave off a small throb. He'd be disappointed when he realized he wasn't getting any action.

And why I was talking about my dick like it had its own mind, I didn't know. Though sometimes he did have his own mind—like the constant hardness he got when I imagined Adrik while alone in my apartment. However, I refused to masturbate over the thought of him. I had to remind myself repeatedly that this was work and Adrik was a client.

Even though it was late again, I could smell something cooking. Didn't Adrik eat dinner at a normal hour? I gripped the basket in front of me and walked into the kitchen to see Adrik standing at the stove with his back to me, stirring something.

A man in the kitchen cooking for you was sexy.

Scratch that. A hot man in the kitchen cooking for you was beyond sexy.

His broad shoulders tapered down to a slim waist, and all of it was covered in another tee. Did this one have a band on it? I'd googled his last one, and it was a rock band from Russia.

"Hi," I called.

Adrik glanced over his shoulder. His eyes slowly grazed over me, and I had the sudden urge to thrust my hips out while my dick shouted, "Look at me. Pay me attention, dammit."

"Jeans," he commented before turning back to the pot.

"Yes." I stepped further in and placed the basket of muffins on the counter. "You said I didn't have to wear a suit, right?" After all, he was in jeans as well. Slightly darker than mine.

"Da." He faced me and eyed the basket, tilting his head to the side before he nodded at it. "What is it?"

"Chocolate muffins. I told you I liked to bake, and I love chocolate muffins. They're my favorite. Maybe it's because my mom never used to make sweet things when I was young, and now that I can, I like to treat myself to these every week. I mean, they'll never be the best in the world, but I think I do all right." I leaned in as if I was about to tell him a secret. "I like to add chocolate sauce to the mix to make them extra gooey." I hummed under my breath. "Then again, not everyone likes gooey like I do." I shrugged. "We'll see if you like them, but after dinner, which smells amazing again. What is it?"

Why did his stare make my blood boil, but in a good way? I felt like a damn teenager with a crush, especially since none of my other clients had brought such a reaction out of me.

Then again, none of them had appealed to me like Adrik did. And I wouldn't say my other clients had been bad-looking either. One was a veterinarian, another a graphic designer, and the other was a lawyer. They weren't old or boring. I had fun with them, but I didn't get fluttery when around them. The nerves were still there, but nothing like I had when I knew I was going back to Adrik's.

Why was he different?

Why couldn't I get him off my mind?

It had to be the accent. It had to be. There was no other reason. He hardly spoke to me. He was gruff, almost looked like he could kill with one look, and was obviously important in the world. Shit, he could even be in the mob, and I wouldn't have a clue.

I scrubbed a hand over my face and silently snorted. I was getting lost in my thoughts too much.

"Zharkoye," he said roughly.

I dropped my hand. "Sorry?" What had we been talking about?

"In the pot. Zharkoye. It is like beef stew."

It sounded good, especially coming out of his mouth. Dang it, I had to stop. I had to pretend he sounded disgusting.

"Well, I'm looking forward to it. Is it nearly ready?"

"Da. Take seat."

"Will do, captain," I teased, and then regretted it when he paused halfway turned back to the stove. Did I apologize? Did he not like people messing with him? Not that it was really messing, I was just trying to be cute.

Note to self: do not be cute with Adrik.

Shifting over to the table, I quickly took my seat. I anxiously bounced my knee up and down and jumped when Adrik set a bowl in front of me.

"Thank you," I told the table.

"Welcome." He took the seat at the head of the table with his own bowl, and we ate in silence. My arch-nemesis.

On the first taste, my mouth orgasmed. At least a part of me was getting action. The stew was melt-in-my-mouth delicious and the meat so tender. "You need to be a chef. Tell me you're a chef. Your meals are amazing, and they can't be just wasted on you and me. Do you cook for your family? Friends? They must rave about how incredible it is."

I clamped my lips closed when I took in his stormy look.

If nut-punching myself wasn't weird, I would do it.

"Sorry," I said softly. "You may have noticed I tend to ramble sometimes. Just… I don't know, shove something in my mouth when I say something you don't like." My eyes bulged out of my head when I realized what I'd said. "I mean a sock or a rag or a towel. Shove something like that in my mouth." Why did I explain that? Now he knew my mind went to the gutter. I could tell he knew. The stormy look faded, and his lips twitched.

"My family is in Russia."

Fuck me in the dark. That was a sentence. I wanted to pat him on the back and say, "Good boy," but I knew it wouldn't go over.

I didn't ask about friends. I already presumed Adrik didn't like to make them. It seemed he kept his private life very private.

I cleared my throat. "That sucks. Well, at least I get to enjoy your cooking." I grinned and went back to eating, ignoring his stare.

We finished dinner, and after I cleared away, I plated two

chocolate muffins. Adrik still sat at the table. He'd been watching me the whole time while I talked about my favorite movies. I dropped a plate in front of him and then sat with my own.

I couldn't help it. I started laughing from his almost fearful look at the dessert. "It's okay. It won't attack." Shaking my head, I smiled. "I'm sure your perfect physique could take a hit for one night. Maybe you could do an extra sit-up for it."

His gaze lifted, along with one brow. "Perfect?"

Shit.

I waved a hand around and pulled my muffin close. "Doesn't matter. Try the muffin. Please?"

He grumbled something but tore off a little from the top and popped it into his mouth. He sucked, chewed, and his eyes lit with something I hadn't seen.

"Good?" I asked, totally searching for compliments.

"Da, perfect."

I didn't care he was teasing by using the word "perfect." I was happy he liked it, and he even went back for more.

After we'd emptied our plates, I stood and went for his plate, but his hand snapped around my wrist, stilling me. My heart went haywire. My eyes drifted to his slightly larger hand on my skin—the skin that warmed from his touch.

"You cooked. I take plates," he explained.

"Right… um, okay." I nodded and swooned on the inside. I plonked back down on my seat, and I couldn't help but notice Adrik slowly drew his hand away. All right, I was hyperaware of his movements, and when he walked by, I—like the stalker I was—took in a deep breath to take in his scent.

Fuck a blender, I had to stop obsessing over this man.

I stood. "Chess?" I yelled and winced.

"Da." His *da* sounded lighter than usual.

"Right, meet you in the living room." I bolted out of the room like my underwear was on fire. I wished this client, Adrik, was more than just company, and that wasn't good. To busy myself, I went to his bookshelf and took a look at the type of books he liked to read. Only to curse under my breath because they were in Russian. Still, I searched for something I recognized.

"Oooh," I mumbled to myself. "What do we have here?" I took a book off the shelf, and my mouth dropped open. It was a popular vampire book. A paranormal *romance* book. One I had read billions of times over. I glanced back to the book-case, but the one in my hand was the only one I could find. Maybe he hadn't enjoyed it as much as I had. That would be tragic, because it was in my top five books of all time. Ones I reread when I was down, and they always brought a smile to my face.

"You have read?"

I screamed from the sound of his voice behind me, dropped the book, and clutched my heart like some damsel in distress. Facing him, I quickly cleared my throat, dropped my hands, and picked up his book.

"Um, yes, I've read it. I've read the whole series; it's one of my favorites. Have you read them all?"

"Nyet, just that."

"Did you like it?"

He shrugged. "It was okay."

I liked this night more than the first because he seemed more talkative. Yet, I still enjoyed being around him when he was silent.

Wait. No, I don't. He's quiet, ugly, and horrible.

Turning back to the bookcase, I replaced the book. While I ran a finger down its spine, I told him, "I'm sure you'd love the other ones. They only get better and better." Stepping back, I smiled at the bookcase. "So many books. Since I'm a lover of reading, of course I checked out a few titles." I laughed, grinning over my shoulder at him. "I didn't understand any of them since they are in Russian."

"Most are. Some are in Spanish."

Wide-eyed, I spun back to him. "You speak Spanish also?"

"Da, and Chinese."

"Holy shit, that's amazing. The only language I know besides English is French, and it's not much." I moved over to sit on the floor near the chess game. "I can count to ten."

"That it?"

Chuckling, I nodded. "Yes. Somehow that stuck with me when I was taught in elementary school."

Adrik sat opposite me again on the couch. He made the first move and then asked, "You want to know some Russian?"

"Yes," I cried a little too enthusiastically.

His lips twitched and he nodded. "What?"

Cocking my head to the side in confusion, I asked as I made my move, "What would I want to know? Do you mean what sayings or words?"

"Da." He nodded, moving his piece.

"Well, I already know *da* means yes and *nyet* means no…. Hmm… okay, how do you say, 'I love chocolate'?" I smiled.

He grinned.

Adrik grinned, and my breath caught in my throat. If I thought he was handsome before, it was nothing when he smiled. Even my stomach tingled at it.

"Ya lyublyu shokolad."

"Fuck," I whispered. He sounded like a wet dream.

"Blyad'."

I slapped a hand over my mouth and laughed. I hadn't thought Adrik had heard me, but obviously, he had. "Seriously?"

"Da." He glanced down and moved. Only, the game was forgotten on my part. I just wanted to lie back and listen to him speak his own language over and over.

"You lose," he stated with a smug smirk an hour later. I wasn't sure what had happened, but something had changed in Adrik, and I liked it a lot. Especially with him smiling and smirking. His eyes even seemed lighter than usual.

"Wait, what?" I looked down and noticed I'd made terrible moves while he distracted me. "That wasn't fair. I wasn't paying attention," I told him with a mock scowl.

"You always need to pay attention," he replied lightly.

I sighed. "Fine, I'll let you have that one. Do we have time for another game?"

His face shut down. The smile vanished. His eyes darkened at the reminder I was there on his money and time. I hated myself for saying anything.

Money was already exchanged before the date even

started, so we didn't have to take cash from the client and make them, or us, feel cheap. But I had a feeling I'd just done it.

He ground his teeth together as he looked down at his watch.

"Nyet," he clipped.

Had the hour and a half already gone by? It was too soon. I didn't want to leave, especially now he was in a mood and it was all my fault.

Adrik stood. "I walk you to lift."

Cry me a damn river. I wanted to cry. It was pathetic… but maybe I could offer to stay on my time?

Grinding my teeth together, I shook my head as I stood. That would be crossing the line. He was a job, after all, and I had to remember it.

Why couldn't I have met him outside of this? Because fucking Sam had been more of a priority than anything or anyone else. Stupid cock-sucking cheating ex. We'd been together only six months, and I'd thought I loved him. Only I knew I didn't since his cheating cut me but didn't gut me. I was only pissed now because I'd wasted those six months on him.

I could have used that time to find Adrik. I snorted silently. Who was I kidding? I wouldn't have met him before now anyway. We obviously ran in different circles. Hell, I still didn't know what he did for a living.

Please don't be a killer or anything illegal.

I lifted my gaze when we reached the elevator. Adrik

pressed the button and shifted to the side with his hand tucked into his jeans.

I went with my urge and reached out, lightly resting my fingers on his forearm. His eyes shot up to mine. I opened my mouth, closed it, and finally said softly, "I really liked dinner. Thank you."

He grunted and nodded. His gaze dropped to my fingers. Even though I was sweating and just about shitting bricks, I left them there. "Next time." I hoped there was a next time. "I'll pay more attention to the game."

The doors to the elevator opened with a ding. I jolted, and my fingers slipped away from his warm skin. I didn't look away from his burning eyes.

"Next time" was all he said before he looked into the elevator.

Next time.

My heart and gut sang "Yay."

"Okay." I stepped away and waved lamely at him. I didn't care that I looked like an idiot, since I saw his lips twitch. "Bye. Have fun. Sleep well," I called as the doors closed.

"*Spokoynoy nochi*, Ben."

"What does that mean?" I yelled, but it was too late; the doors had fully closed. And I wasn't sure, but I thought I heard a deep chuckle. I really needed to learn Russian. I also wanted to press the button to the penthouse again and go back up to ask him to call me by my real name.

Dangerous.

Being around Adrik was more than dangerous because I... I really didn't want him as my client. I wanted to know everything about him outside of work. Again, I wasn't sure what it was about him, but I craved his attention. Nothing like I had before. Shit, I hardly knew the guy, and the conversations we'd had that night were the longest we'd shared.

I was going crazy.

Or I just needed to get laid.

Maybe I could talk to Lucas about it. We'd become close in the last few months, and I knew with not only Lucas but our new friend Kylo, I could share anything I wanted. However, Lucas was in a new relationship, and I didn't want him to worry about me and my stupid thoughts. It would have to be Kylo I spoke with, and since he also worked for Polished, he might know where I was coming from. Still, it would have to wait. I had another client tomorrow, and I needed to study my ass off for class.

I would push Adrik to the back of my mind.

I would treat him like any other client—friendly, but keep my distance.

There'd be no more talking about myself. My real personal life. I would have to think of a story for Ben's new life and stick to it. Since I'd already shared I was studying medicine, I couldn't go back on that.

As the doors opened, the guards looked over, both scowling. I pasted a smile on my face and made my way to the doors with a cheerful "Goodnight." Of course they didn't reply. I exited out the doors and into the cool night.

Death appeared out of nowhere, and I hate to admit it, but I squealed like a girl, causing him to laugh.

"No issues?" he asked, smirking.

"Nope, smooth sailing like last time."

"Good. You got another tonight? I couldn't remember, and my fuckin' phone went flat while the goddamn charger is broken. Well, now it is."

I shook my head. "Sounds like it's not your night, and yes, it's only this one. I'm heading home."

"I'll follow you."

Rolling my eyes, I said, "You don't—"

"I'm following."

"Okay. Thank you, and see you next time."

He tipped his chin up to me, and apparently, that was his reply. He turned and stalked to his car. Smiling, I suddenly felt more comfortable from my little pep talk earlier.

I would put Adrik in the client bubble, and that was it.

As soon as I googled what he'd said in Russian.

I wasn't sure what happened to me over the two weeks before our next appointment. But my little talk to myself went out the window. Worse. Adrik kept popping into my mind, even when I jerked off. I tried pushing him out, but no matter who I pictured, it would morph into Adrik, which had me coming instantly.

I'd kept myself busy with other clients, school, studying, and helping Lucas move into the house he and Wreck got, but it wasn't enough, obviously. I even visited a bookstore to buy the rest of the series for Adrik. The books were bundled in my arms. Death had given me a weird look about the gift, but he didn't say anything. I wished he had. Maybe then I would have seen some sense and kept the parcel in the car or thrown it out the window. Only books weren't meant to be treated like that. I could have kept them for myself and had two sets of them or given them to Lucas and Wreck as a present.

Shit, why hadn't I thought of that before?

I glanced to the shrubbery beside the doors and considered hiding them before I went in. I'd collect them on the way out, but I worried the guards would think I was planting a bomb or something and shoot me before asking.

Taking a deep breath, I placed the wrapped book pile under one arm and opened the door. As I stepped through, the guards looked over. One grunted and nodded toward the elevator. With a smile, I made my way there and pressed the button. It now seemed like the guards weren't worried about me. I could have gotten away with hiding the books, damn it.

My stomach kicked up its fluttering when the doors opened, and I stepped into the elevator. I knew there were cameras; I'd seen them. It meant I couldn't drop the books and rest my hands on my knees while I hyperventilated.

Stupid books. Stupid me for being nice.

The ride up went too fast, and when I stepped into the condo, I knew Adrik wouldn't be waiting, so I quickly made my way into the kitchen before my nerves got the better of me and I hid in the closet.

The lack of scent hit me as soon as I reached the kitchen and didn't find Adrik in there. He wasn't cooking. Had I gone on about his food being amazing too much, and it put him off? Or was it the mention of cooking for his family that had done it?

Dear God, why did he want me back if he didn't like what I said? Again, I'd been surprised when Country told me I was coming back and that Adrik had booked me for the next two months on every second weekend. I acted cool when he'd said it, but on the inside, I was throwing rainbow glitter all around while dancing and singing.

Which wasn't a good sign. I was too happy to come back.

Although I wasn't so sure, because with Adrik not cooking, what did it mean? What would we be doing? I doubted having a deep and meaningful chat would be on the cards.

I placed the books on the counter and stilled when I heard pounding footsteps in the house. Could he have forgotten I was coming?

Adrik turned into the kitchen with his phone in hand. He took my breath away. He wore a dark blue suit with a white shirt under it. "We eat out," he stated. His eyes landed on the wrapped present, and he stopped still.

"So… um, I got you a little something. It's only small…. Well, it looks big, but really the…. If you don't like it, I'll take it and give it to a friend… but you might like it." His gaze lifted to mine, and my lips snapped shut because intensity filled his eyes.

He moved to the counter and unwrapped the gift in seconds. The pile of books slid to the side.

"I thought you might like the rest of the series. Just remember with each one, they do get better. *I* thought so anyway, and I also found at the end one, I still craved more, but I don't think the author will be doing another."

His jaw clenched. He breathed roughly, causing his nostrils to flare.

"Ty tak dobr. Spasibo za etot dobryy podarok."

"Sorry?" I asked, not understanding a word since I hadn't

magically learned Russian. Okay, I had started to study it online, but he spoke so quickly I didn't pick up on one word.

"Thank you," he said. I was sure that wasn't all he'd said, but I wasn't going to ask again.

"You're welcome." I smiled. When he didn't say anything and he wouldn't stop looking at the books, I asked, "Where are we going for dinner?"

"Somewhere."

"Okay," I drew out. "Way to be cryptic."

His grin clutched my heart and warmed my body completely. Not good.

"Come," he ordered, and turned. We made our way to the elevator, where he pressed the button, and since I hadn't long arrived, the doors opened straightaway.

Stepping in, I queried, "Am I wearing the appropriate clothes for this mystery place?"

"Da" was all he said before typing something in his phone. Okay then, I guess where we were going wasn't too fancy.

Panic took me, and I pulled my own phone free. **West: We're on the move. He's taking me out to dinner.**

Death: Where?

West: I don't know. I think he wants it to be a surprise.

"Tell your guard he can follow. It will be safe where we are going," Adrik said.

"Um… you know about him?"

He stared down at me. "Da. My men have seen him. It is good to know they take care of their people."

I nodded with a warm smile. "They do. They're great like

that." I glanced back down to the phone. **Death: This is not good. I'll call in more people.**

I quickly typed out: **No need. Adrik said you can follow, and it's safe where we're going.**

The doors dinged just as Death replied with: **Since he knows about me, I want clearance to wherever we're going.**

"Adrik?"

He glanced over his shoulder as we made our way to the guards waiting by the front doors. "Um, my guard would like clearance to wherever we're going."

He nodded. "He will have it."

"Sir, are you sure about taking—"

"Do not ask question again, Leonid."

Leonid dropped his gaze. "Yes, sir."

They scrambled to open the doors when Adrik started for them. We went outside, and I saw Death already sitting and waiting in his car. Adrik slipped into the back of a damn limousine. I refrained from clapping in glee at my first ride and climbed in after him.

Glancing around with what I knew would be a huge smile, I stopped on Adrik, who watched me. "This is cool. I've never been in a limo and always wanted to go in one. I'd thought about hiring one for prom. I had it all planned out," I told him as the limo started driving, and I opened the mini refrigerator at the side to see bottles of water and champagne. "I was going to ask the guy I'd been crushing on for years to prom. He'd be ecstatic and fall in love with me, and we'd get matching suits and have a dream night." I snorted out a laugh, leaning back into the seat, which was super comfortable. "It didn't work out that way. The guy punched me in the face, called me a faggot, and told me if I showed my face at prom, he and his buddies would kick my ass." Shrugging, I added, "I hadn't thought my dream would crash, especially when it was about a month before that I'd seen a friend of his giving him head in his car in the parking lot." I chuckled. At least I was able to laugh at it now. "Still, I had a good night. I went out to my first gay club."

Oh shit… there I went again, telling the man things about my real life.

"What is his name?"

I jerked back at the venom in his voice. "What?"

"His name. Tell me," he clipped.

Whoa, okay. If I had to guess, Adrik was pissed on my behalf and might have the idea to hunt this guy down to kill him. That wasn't good.

I laughed nervously. "Adrik." I shook my head, scooted a little closer, and put my hand on his knee. "It's fine. I'm over it, and I'm sure wherever he is, karma has fucked him hard for being a douche."

Adrik's gaze was on my hand. He grunted, jaw clenching. "You won't give me name?"

"No, sorry." God, why was I apologizing for saving someone? It was weird, yet my chest expanded and warmed because it was then I knew Adrik cared.

Shit.

I removed my hand and waved it around. "Anyway, can I get a hint as to where we're going?" My heart was beating so fast in my chest. I didn't need to know Adrik was protective or sweet in an aggressive way, because knowing it made him more appealing.

"Nyet," Adrik said softly. He smirked over at me. "You do not like surprises?"

"They're great… for other people."

He snorted.

"Is it far?" I tried.

He crossed his arms and kept his smirk in place.

Rolling my eyes, I huffed. "Fine."

"How is college?"

This was normal. Too normal. Like a couple seeing how their day was. I wanted to cry because my heart wanted it to be real.

Brushing invisible lint off my jeans, I shrugged. "College is college. Hard, but something needed for the future."

"Had you always wanted to be a doctor?"

I smiled. "Pretty much. My mind is inquisitive. I love puzzles of any kind, and besides helping people, I knew becoming a doctor would be a good challenge."

"You will practice in a… doctor's office?"

"Yes, being a surgeon wouldn't be for me. I get a little queasy with blood."

When he chuckled, it drew my attention immediately. He looked beautiful laughing like that. He shook his head. "You will still need to deal with blood."

Smiling, I shrugged. "I know, but not as much."

I liked this. Talking with him.

Too much.

Sadness gripped me for a moment, but I pushed it away. *Client, client, client,* I chanted in my head. Hell, Adrik probably thought nothing of our time together anyway. I was behaving like a lovestruck teen with a silly little crush. I had to put my man pants on and stop this shit.

"We are here," Adrik said.

Pushing everything aside, I grinned and shifted over to the window to look out. My eyes widened. "A casino?"

"Da."

"We're going into a casino for dinner?"

"Da." He grinned.

"Well, I certainly didn't expect that," I told him when we pulled into the underground parking. We were lucky enough to get a spot right in front of the doors and one that would fit a limo…. Wait, how were we so lucky? I laughed at myself. Of course we were lucky. Adrik probably paid them to save a spot.

Our door opened, and I jumped since I was looking at Adrik. He was still grinning, and if I was right, I had a feeling I was missing something.

"Ready, sir?"

"Da," Adrik answered and nodded at me.

I climbed out, and nerves rolled through to my stomach when I saw Death parked in a spot next to our car. He got out of his and shut the door just as Adrik stepped up behind me.

"Do you wish to follow or stay here?" Adrik asked. I thought he was asking me, but I saw his gaze on Death when I looked over my shoulder.

"I'll follow."

"Come then," he ordered. His men, and somehow he'd gathered four more, spread out. Two went ahead. Another two stayed with us as we made our way in, and the last kept a distance behind us. Death followed a little closer than what they were.

Adrik and I walked side by side, but I stopped and took in the view when we entered.

"Holy shit," I whispered. Lights and noise bombarded me. There were people everywhere, and even though it looked like this was the only floor, which was huge on its own, I'd seen from the outside it was at least twenty stories high.

My view caught on Adrik, who stood a couple of paces in front of me and looked back at me with a soft smile. One I hadn't seen before. One that caused my dick to throb.

Fuck.

"Sorry," I said, catching up to him. "Even when I turned legal and we weren't far from all this, I never went to a casino."

"Never?" he asked, surprise evident in his voice.

"Nyet," I said, and grinned over at him as we walked.

His gaze was in front of us, but I didn't miss his smile.

"I never felt the need to. Life kept me busy, and there was also me saving every penny I had for college, books, and rent."

We stopped at a row of elevators. "Your parents, they helped?"

"In elementary and high school, yes. But not for college. It was lucky I got a scholarship, but they didn't like I moved away from them, so they weren't… um, forthcoming in helping when I could have gone to a community college where they were and lived at home."

Goddamn it. I was sharing again. Telling him too much. I glanced behind me to see Death was closer, and his brows were pinched. He was also frowning.

Why could I hold myself, my real self, back with other clients but not with Adrik? There was something about him that made me want to share the real me.

The doors before us opened, and we stepped in with two guards and Death. Did I need to introduce Death to him? It felt weird he was there, but I didn't know if Death would want me to share his name, his biker name, with them.

"It must have been hard," Adrik said.

What was?

My dick?

I glanced down and noted I didn't sport a hard-on, but there was a slight bulge.

Death snorted and covered it with a cough.

Oh crap, what had we been talking about? Right, my parents, college. With a burning face, I met Adrik's amused gaze in the mirror in front of us and said, "To start off with, yes. But when I realized I had my freedom, I loved it and made sure it worked."

We stepped off onto a floor. I didn't take notice of which number, though. The guards retook their positions, and I walked beside Adrik. This floor seemed more salubrious, and I really felt underdressed.

I leaned closer to Adrik. "I feel out of place here. You should have told me to wear a suit."

He stopped and faced me. "I noted the first time you wore one, you seemed uncomfortable."

"Um, I was a bit, but I'd still wear one for places like this."

"You are with me. You do not need to worry."

Stupid heartwarming words.

Ignore them, West.

I shrugged at him. "Okay."

He studied me for a moment and nodded. Before we could walk further, two women appeared in front of us.

The blonde clapped and beamed up at Adrik, who frowned. "You're Adrik Hail, right? The owner of this casino?"

The owner?

Adrik owned this place.

No wonder he told me not to worry about what I was wearing.

"Da," Adrik clipped.

"Da? What does 'da' mean?" They giggled.

"You're very good-looking," the brunette added with a slight slur to her words. Great, they were drunk.

"We would love to keep you company for the night." The blonde winked.

Adrik's nostrils flared. I had a feeling he was about to sic his guards on them or verbally abuse some paying customers.

Just as the blonde reached for Adrik's arm, I took her hand and pulled both of their attention onto me. I smiled wide. "That's really sweet of you two beauties to offer, but Mr. Hail is very busy tonight." I glanced around and saw Leonid. I waved him over. Thankfully, he listened even if he glared at me. "Leonid here would love to get you ladies a couple of free drinks to make up for declining your lovely offer."

"I will not leave—"

"Sdelay eto," Adrik bit out. Whatever he'd said caused Leonid to stiffen and nod.

"Please, come this way." He waved toward one of the bar areas.

"That's so nice," they both cooed before they followed Leonid with a final wave to us.

I jumped when a hand landed on the small of my back. "Come," Adrik said, his tone softer than it had been.

My skin tingled along with my balls from his touch. Even when it was innocent, I couldn't control the extra beat in my heart or the small stumble I took as we walked. Adrik was kind enough to ignore my clumsiness.

At another set of elevators, we stopped. Adrik turned back and said, "You can all stay here."

"Where will you take him?" Death asked.

"Up to my office, where we will have dinner."

"One hour," Death said.

I stiffened. Adrik hated the reminder of our time. But all he did was nod, face the elevator, and swipe a card through the panel beside it. The doors opened, and his hand was back, teasing my body.

It really wasn't good that I wanted to feel his hands on my skin. To have them run over my body like he wanted to consume me.

Fuck me with a double dildo. I really was screwed with my feelings for this man.

How could it be so?

Why after only three meetings with him?

Why him to begin with?

Maybe it had to do with him opening up to me slowly, very slowly, each time we were together. I never thought he'd own a casino. Hell, he might own more than one. But... I didn't care about what he had. I cared about who he was on the inside—

Fuck me, please someone come along and shoot me in the head because I sound like a total smitten dickhead from a love story.

Only this love story wouldn't have a happy ending. I'd have a broken heart, because Adrik Hail was and would always be a client.

Shaking my head, I'd come to the decision I needed to get my ass into gear and really talk to someone about how I was feeling. I also needed to pay attention to the now.

In the elevator, I asked lightly, "Do you always get women offering themselves up to you?"

"Mostly. Some men as well."

I choked when I sucked in a sharp breath. "Really?"

He smiled, and a small "Da" slipped from between his lips.

Lips I had to stop staring at. I lifted my gaze and quickly turned to face the front because I'd been caught. I was grateful the doors opened. Stepping off, I glanced around. Half the room was made up of windows. I went straight over to them.

"Wow," I stated. The view was of the floor we'd just been on. Men, women, workers, tables, poker machines, bars, drinks, food… I could see everything.

"Do you like?" Adrik asked from beside me.

I laughed. "If I owned this, I wouldn't want to leave. But then again, I'm a people watcher. I could sit in a coffee shop and just watch people. And, oh my goodness, that sounds like I'm a creep." I grabbed his upper arm. "I promise I'm not some stalker or killer."

Adrik chuckled. "I know."

I smiled. "So," I drew out. "You own this place."

His gaze went back out the window. I took mine there also and rested my hands on the windowsill. "Da. This and two others. I bought them when I moved here."

"Wow again. That's pretty impressive, but it must keep you very busy?"

"I like busy."

But did he? I saw the dip to his brows when he said it. My stomach twisted for him because I honestly didn't think he was happy. Why would a man in his prime want to hire an escort for company when he could obviously get anyone he wanted? It was hard to guess the reasons, but it did have me wondering what went on the receipt when a client hired an escort.

Was Adrik hiding his sexuality?

Did he have parents like my own who didn't accept it?

I hoped one day my parents would, but they were highly against homosexuality since God apparently never created us that way.

I wanted to ask about Adrik's but knew I couldn't. "Maybe one day you'll get to settle down a little." I bumped my hip into his. "For now, I'm starving, and things could get ugly if I'm not fed soon."

His lips twitched. "It'll be delivered soon."

I looked around me. "Do you have telepathy? I didn't see you tell or ring anyone?"

"They would have seen me arrive. I ordered for you." He winced. He actually winced. Worried I wouldn't want him to take control, maybe?

I would not think about him taking control in the bedroom.

I wouldn't.

Shit, it was in there now, and I had to abort the thought quickly because Adrik was staring at me like I'd lost it. Which was a possibility.

I cleared my throat. "No, that's fine… I'll eat anything, really. As long as it's not anything with pineapple." I screwed up my nose. "I hate that stuff."

"On pizza?"

"Yes! People who have it on pizza are monsters."

With a laugh, he waved me over to a table I hadn't seen. "I eat on pizza."

I went to sit down and nearly missed the seat, which caused Adrik to chuckle some more. "You don't."

"Not really. I do not eat pizza."

My jaw dropped. "You don't eat pizza?"

He shook his head, smiling.

I blinked. Adrik had heard me rave about it, only for me to discover he didn't consume the best thing on earth besides chocolate muffins…. I was at a loss for words.

"We're changing that," I stated.

He quirked a brow. "We are?"

"Hell yes, we are. Next time we're going to get pizza for dinner, and I'm going to watch you eat it. Okay, that sounds creepy, but you know what I mean."

He chuckled. "Da."

There was a buzz, and Adrik stood and walked over to a massive desk to press something. "That desk is huge."

He faced me and stared. I said desk, right?

"You do not like?" he asked.

We were still talking about his desk, *right?*

"I'm suddenly confused," I admitted.

He stared some more. Until he must have registered what *I'd* been thinking and grinned, shaking his head at me. "I like big things."

I snorted.

He glowered, but the venom of it wasn't there. "Big *work* areas."

"Whatever floats your boat," I teased.

He stalked toward me, rested one hand on the table in front of me and the other on the back of my seat. He leaned in close. I ate my heart since it had jumped into my mouth, excited by his close attention.

"What does this mean? Floats your boat?" His voice, his damn voice, was low and husky, and I wanted to drink it.

Weird thought, but my mind had been lost since he neared me. It was then I realized before tonight, I had been the only one to get close, to reach out. First, it had been with the touch to my back, and now this. He was blooming in front of me. Showing me the real him.

Yet, a part of my brain still asked me if he was actually gay. My other clients had been flirty. Adrik hadn't… until now, but was this flirting?

"Have I broken you?"

"Yes, no… what was the question?"

Heavens, he was looking at my lips.

A ding sounded, and the spell was broken. Adrik straightened as the doors opened, and he started toward the waitress who stepped out.

"I could fall for you," I whispered to myself. I could. Easily. And that scared me, as there was a high risk of being hurt.

My jaw hurt from clenching it. It was fucking strange that I suddenly wanted to cry. What was wrong with me?

I heard Adrik say something to the waitress. I glanced over to see her nod and move back into the elevator, leaving the cart behind. Once the doors were closed, Adrik pushed the food our way.

He was handsome.

He was scary.

He was gruff.

Sweet.

Reserved.

Funny.

But never would he be mine.

When would I get that through my thick head?

He was a client.

I worked for an escort service and was paid to spend time with this addictive man.

My chest cracked. I had to stop. I had to. For my sake, for my feelings, my heart, my sanity, because if I didn't, I wouldn't be able to stay away.

I had two weeks to get my head around what I was feeling. After tonight, I wouldn't see him for two weeks. In that time, I would talk to Kylo for some advice, and then I would either cancel Adrik as a client or continue this torture on myself.

Why did I have to get feelings for him?

A gentle pinch to my chin had me raising my gaze to Adrik's concerned one. "Where are you?"

I forced a smile. "Here in your office."

He studied me, and under his assessing gaze, it felt like I had everything open for him to see. My mind, my body, and my soul. He shook his head as his thumb slowly caressed my skin under my chin.

Oh boy, I wanted to melt into him. I wanted to wrap my arms around his waist and tell him my name and everything about me. How I didn't want to work and get paid for his company. I wanted him to give it to me, and I'd have it freely.

"Your mind is miles away."

I scraped my top teeth over my bottom lip and once more threw my thoughts and worries aside to live in the moment. To enjoy Adrik Hail. I grinned. "Sorry, I have a test coming up at college, and the worry got the best of me for a moment." The lie felt wrong, but it had to be done.

Adrik's brows dipped. Eventually, he nodded. "I would help, but I do not know how."

Breathe. I did so as my heart clenched tightly.

"You are, by taking my mind off the worry."

He tapped my chin and went to the trays. "Let us eat. You seem to enjoy food."

Chuckling, I replied, "I sure do."

The time went too fast. All too soon, I was back in the underground parking lot with guards surrounding us. I was getting a lift back with Death, since the date had ended. I felt sick, but I still looked around to Adrik as he waited beside the limo and smiled. His lips twitched.

I got into the car with a lame wave, and Death backed out of the space. Adrik surprised me by staring back at me. I didn't look away until we were out of sight from him.

Leaning back in the seat, I sighed. Then realized and voiced, "The car's at the condo."

"Already organized someone to pick it up."

I nodded, taking my gaze out the side window. Lost in thought. Lost in what I would do. My heart called for me to stay, keep at it, then at least I would get to see him. My mind was a different story. It shouted at me to stop my stupidity and get my ass into gear by ending this. So, maybe it was time to listen to my mind to save my heart. It was probably a good idea to cancel our appointments before my feelings grew into something more. All I had at the moment was a mild crush—yes, I would keep telling myself that—and attraction.

"West!" Death called a little harshly, making me think he'd been trying to get my attention for a while.

"Sorry, lost in the clouds. What did you say?"

"I asked if you were all right?"

I huffed a laugh. "I'm fine."

Death made a noise in the back of his throat. He didn't buy my bullshit, but I couldn't tell him I was catching feelings for a client.

"How was your night?" Death asked.

He never asked.

I shrugged. "Good. It was the first time I've been in a casino. Never had time before."

"The client seemed to take a liking to you."

I forced a laugh. "Don't they all." Every client I'd had so far wanted more time with me. Which was good for the pocket.

"Mr. Hail…. Never mind."

"What?" I asked.

Death shrugged. "Was just gonna comment that Mr. Hail brings you out of your shell more than the others."

I tensed. "What do you mean by that?"

"Just that with the other clients, you act polite and sweet and shit, but you're more yourself around that guy we just left."

Huh, I'd never noticed before. Could it be true? I shook my head. "I don't think so."

"I'd never seen you with him before, but I have the others since they take you out. Just looked different to me, but I could be wrong."

He was. He had to be. I wouldn't let my walls down that much around a client.

Fuck me, who was I kidding? Only myself, apparently. With the other clients, I stuck with a story of Ben. I didn't tell them about myself, my real life. Death was right, damn it. I just didn't want to admit it to myself.

Again, it told me I was in too deep with Adrik. I'd gotten feelings attached to the job. What hurt the most was that if I did choose to not see Adrik again, he wouldn't know why. He wouldn't know it was because of me and that my decision had nothing to do with him. Could I tell him? No, I didn't think it would be wise. He'd only see I was weak. Adrik was the type of man who needed someone strong to stand by his side, and me? I was running. Running because I couldn't do one job right and not get attached to a client.

If I did run.

I really needed to talk to Kylo. Maybe he was in the same position I was in with a client. I hoped so. I wouldn't feel like such a dickhead.

A thought flew into my mind.

"Death?"

"Yeah?"

"When a client books in someone and pays, what does the company show on the record?"

"A computer technician company."

Huh. It looked like Adrik's transactions were hidden if anyone looked into him. Which would be good for a person who didn't want people to know he was gay… or into guys as well as girls. I wasn't sure which category Adrik fell into; we never went into it. Of course, my new train of thought took me to a place where I could justify my choice of ending things. *If* I did. It could also mean Adrik didn't want a real relationship with a man. Eventually, he would settle with a woman to keep the image of a straight, obviously loaded businessman. Hell, he could own more than just the casinos, and if he wanted to expand, it was no secret gay people were still treated as pariahs, which no doubt would be more challenging when it came to business. Shit, even my parents frowned upon homosexuality because of their interpretation of religion.

It didn't matter that He, my god, loved me for who I was, not who I took to bed. Not that I could ever tell them that.

Sighing, I pinched the bridge of my nose and leaned back into the seat. A headache pounded at me. I was thinking too much, but my mind was just a ball of confusion.

Right, I would make a plan.

I'd keep myself busy with schooling, work, and friends. I'd catch up with Kylo without Lucas. Since Lucas was in his bubble of happiness, I didn't want to rain on it by talking about the mess I'd made of things. I also had to look for another place to stay since my lease was up soon and I hated the new neighbors who'd moved in.

"West?"

I groaned and flopped my head Death's way. "Did I miss something again?"

He grinned. "We're here."

I straightened and looked out the window. Shit, that was fast. "Sorry, got a headache coming on."

"Want me to walk you in?"

Grinning, I reached out and patted his arm. "Aren't you sweet, but I'll be fine."

His lips thinned. "Take care, yeah?"

I opened the door and climbed out. "Will do, you too."

He snorted. I waved and shut the door. It was time for some relaxation. A shower and then sleep sounded like heaven, and maybe if I kept singing a song in my mind, I wouldn't think about Adrik before I fell asleep.

Look at that, I just made a fucking funny.

CHAPTER FIVE
ADRIK

I gripped the phone when the words registered. "Mr. Hail, this is Saint, co-owner from Polished. Unfortunately, Ben is no longer available. Would you like to reschedule with someone else?"

Anger burned through my gut, but then fear overtook me, and I asked, "Is he good?" I refused to use his business name. I especially hated it when I had to use it in person with West. After our first meeting, I had known his real name when one of my men, the only one I trusted, had done a little digging.

"He is."

Obviously, that was all he would give me. I wanted to know why. I wanted to know everything.

Through clenched teeth, I asked, "Will he be available for next weekend as usual?" I was foolish and thought West would want to see me a week early to make up for this missed time, but Saint's next words told me just how pathetic I had been.

"Unfortunately, no, sorry. If you go to our website, we have more men online for you to view. I'll just have to give you the password to access them."

He was done with me.

Why?

What had changed?

I could fall for you. Those words had played in my mind over and over. Words I was not meant to hear.

"Nyet," I clipped in my own language. Trying again, since this Saint could be a fool and have it wrong, I asked, "I would prefer Ben. Is he working with your company still?" West may have canceled all his other clients and moved from the business altogether. It was what I hoped for.

"He does, for now, but the hours he'd been doin' aren't suitin' him any longer."

Blyad'. "I'll take any hour he has available." I regretted those words as soon as they were out of my mouth. I sounded desperate.

"I'm sorry, but that won't be possible. He's already been booked out for the next month with his new hours."

I did not believe him. I straightened in my chair in my fucking cold office as the anger flamed once more.

He did not want me.

Was there another?

"Will he be sleeping with these other clients?" I bit out.

"It's no business of yours what my employee does," Saint snarked back.

"Fine. Give me the access code, and I'll take a look, then get back to you." As soon as he gave the code to me, I hung up.

Even though I wrote the code down, I would not use it, because West had crawled under my skin and was stuck there.

"Dimitri," I barked.

My door opened, and my true friend stepped through. "*Da, Adrik?*" He closed the door and came closer as I ripped off the piece of paper, screwed it up, and threw it into the bin beside my obnoxiously large desk.

In Russian, I said, "*West. Keep an eye on him.*"

He replied in the same, "*What happened?*"

"*I do not know, but I am no longer his client.*" I clenched my teeth as I stood and strode to the window. It had been only one week since West had stood here with me. He had seemed to want to be here. He had acted calm, sweet, and nervous. Like all the times before. What had changed?

Had someone said something?

Had someone upset him?

I did not like this change at all.

"*I'll get a few of my men to watch him.*"

"*Men you trust.*"

"*Of course.*" He stopped beside me and leaned his shoulder into the window. I could feel his stare.

Sighing, I barked in English, "What?"

"*You have had other men before. None you've paid for. So, what is it about him?*"

What was it about West Millbrook that I wanted an eye on him? That I could not stop thinking about him.

It was simple.

I needed him.

I needed West to breathe. To smile. To lighten my life.

There was no other who had captured my attention in seconds like West had. As Dimitri said, I had been with other men, not many, but enough to know I preferred them. But none of them had my cock aching, my heart beating, and my soul lightening like West.

I never thought it would come from someone I paid to spend time with. But it had, and I hadn't even fucked him. I was glad I'd made the choice to hire an escort for the first time instead of going to the trouble of finding someone to keep me company. It was on my terms and with someone who knew I wasn't looking at dating them.

That went to hell when West walked in and his nerves got the best of him, causing him to ramble. I never thought I would find it endearing. But I had. What helped was the attraction I felt for the younger man. He wore a suit and even when he seemed uncomfortable in it, he still looked appealing.

He was not much shorter than me, smaller in body, and cuter than I would usually go for. But I liked it. Him. A lot.

It worried me I wanted to spend more time with him. He had walked into my home and charmed me like I had never been before. His looks, his personality, his generosity, everything about him had captured me from the first moment.

"Adrik?"

"If you spent time with him, you would see. He is smart, caring, hardworking…." I shrugged. *"Everything about him appeals to me like no other."*

Dimitri whistled. *"Sounds like love."* I rolled my eyes.

Dimitri went on. *"Why do you not chase him then? Why not date him?"*

Facing him, I glared. *"You know why."*

Dimitri sighed, and as I looked back out the window, his hand dropped to my shoulder. *"Your father is in Russia. His associates are there also. I am sure he would want you to be happy. No matter who it is with. I know you also fear that the one you love will only want you for your money and connections, but I do not see that from West."*

I did not either. Still, I said nothing, because I could not find the words. My father loved me. This I knew. As did my mother. But the world around them was complicated. I left because I wanted out. That life did not interest me. The business side of things had, which was why I had my own away from my father and the family name, Mikhaillova. Before I left Russia, I changed my last name to Hail. I could not have people connect me to my father's business. I never would be a part of the *mafiya*. That was my father. He was the one in control of the mafia in Russia.

Dimitri groaned. His hand dropped, and he said, *"You are just as stubborn as he is. Tell your parents when they visit who you are. You will see, they will still love you."* He made his way toward the door.

Fuck. He had to remind me of their visit. I did want to see them, but my mood had soured ever since that phone call.

"Dimitri—"

"I know, I know. I will make sure the man you want will be watched."

"Thank you, friend."

He tapped the doorframe. *"You know anything for you,"* he said before he left, shutting the door behind him.

Dimitri and I had been friends since we attended school together. I trusted him more than I trusted my own brothers. Brothers who my father would leave the business to. Another reason I'd moved. Not that I cared; they were older and would inherit the business before I did. Where I was vicious and ruthless when I had to be, they were all the time. My parents witnessed this when I wouldn't kill a man for stealing from me after I'd discovered he had just wanted to feed his family. My "kindness" could have been why they "allowed" me to move to the United States.

I didn't see the point in killing for the name. To put fear in others. I wanted reasons for it, evidence first.

Instead, I killed if anyone threatened my family and friends. I killed to protect. My hands had been bloody on many occasions. The dirtiness did not bother me when it came to protecting me, mine, and what I'd built for my life.

People here were figuring out I didn't sit back and take shit. I would fight. I would make blood spray if needed, and what they thought never bothered me, as long as it meant they would leave me alone in the end.

I thought I liked being alone. I had Dimitri, a friend I could not see life without.

I didn't need a companion—a lover.

I was happy. Content.

Then West walked in, and I second-guessed my choice. I *wanted* someone by my side. I *wanted* someone to come home to. And I wanted that *someone* to be him. It surprised me how quickly he had captured me. With that being said, I hadn't met anyone like him, so I could not have known I would hold feelings for the man in such a short amount of time.

Usually, I preferred dark-haired men with blue eyes. Yet, I did not care that West had blond hair with topaz eyes. Because they were eyes I wanted to stare into all the time. He had a mouth I wanted to take with mine. And a body that was made for me to touch, to hold, to fuck.

I could fall for you.

He had said it. I did not imagine it. Why would he say something like that and then call off our time together? Had it to do with someone, or was there a possibility West was scared about feeling the same way I did? Consumed by one another?

Khristos. A thrill rolled through my gut at the thought.

The phone on my desk started ringing. I wanted to ignore it, but a distraction could be a good idea, or I would end up on West's doorstep to his shitty little apartment to demand the reason for dropping me.

I stalked over to the desk and answered sharply with "Da?"

"Moy syn," my mother said into the phone in Russian before she switched to English to add, "I have been trying to call your mobile."

Moving around the desk, I picked up my phone. "Sorry, Mama, I had it on silent. Is everything all right?"

"Da, I just wanted to see how my boy is."

"Good. Work always keeps me busy."

"*Stupid work,*" she spat in Russian and continued in our home language. "*It always keeps all my boys busy. I'm looking forward to seeing you, Adrik. Tell me, do you have someone to intro-duce to your mama and papa when we come?"*

"No, Mama, no one special. As I said, work keeps me occupied too much to have a life outside of it."

She fell silent. Which couldn't be good.

Of course, an image of West dropped into my mind. The one of him standing before the counter where he placed his gift for me while blushing.

My chest ached.

I had wanted to take him into my arms and claim his mouth. No one other than my parents or Dimitri had given me a gift outside of my birthday. It pleased me too much. As did his chocolate muffins.

Shaking my head, I called, "Mama?"

"You sound sad, *moy mal'chik.*" My boy. Out of her sons, I had been the only one who she called her boy. I never asked and she never explained why.

I tensed. *"I am fine, Mama. Tired, maybe."*

"Nyet, there is something else."

"I don't know what to tell you, Mama. Nothing has happened."

She huffed, and then I heard her cover the phone and have a muffled conversation. I knew who would be nearby. My parents' love was strong, and they never strayed far from one another.

There was a shuffle, and then through the line was my father. *"Adrik, we're moving up our trip and will be there next week. Do not bother with a hotel. I know you have some free condos you have not leased out in your building. We will stay in one of those."*

"*Papa, tell Mama you do not need to move your trip forward. She worries for nothing.*"

"*Are you crazy? I cannot tell her that. She worries, I worry. She wants, I give. You will learn this when you find your one.*"

Sighing, I scrubbed a hand over my face. "*I will see you next week then. Text me when you have the details, and I'll pick you up at the airport. And Papa—*"

"*Do not fear, son. No one from here will know we are traveling. No harm will follow. You think I am stupid now? I would not risk my jewel or my son who wants nothing to do with the business.*"

"*Papa—*"

"*Forget it. I am already getting the evil eye from your mama for saying this. I understand. Some days, I even wish I was as smart as you and got out when I could. It is too late and anyway, I will give it over to Michail soon. Then it will be his problem. Then your mama and I will visit more. Six months has been too long.*"

"*It has. I look forward to seeing you both.*"

"*Talk soon.*"

"*Yes,*" I replied and hung up.

At least there was one good thing about my parents' early arrival; it would distract me enough until I found out more about West. It could also save me from approaching him and making a fool of myself.

Now that I thought about it, there was a possibility I'd misheard his words that night.

West may not feel anything for me, and I—

No. I heard those words, and I would find out what happened, why West stopped our time together. Eventually. It may take time, but I was confident our paths would cross, and when they did, I would not let West slip through my fingers again.

I would make sure I hadn't imagined our connection.

And when I did, I would make him mine.

It also meant I had to listen to Dimitri and tell my parents exactly who I was.

*J*clenched my jaw when I saw Kylo in the hospital bed. Kylo, who Lucas and I had become fast friends with, worked at Polished. He'd been attacked by his biological father. Not only that, he'd witnessed his father shoot his mother before they beat Kylo for money. I never wanted to hurt a person more than I did Kylo's dad when I found out. Unfortunately, he was still on the run, and since Kylo was a member of the Diamond MC, the club would do everything in their power to find the… the fucker, and rain justice down on him like he deserved.

"Are you just gonna stare at me all day or come here and give me a hug?" Kylo asked.

"Don't fuckin' touch him for too long, though," Saint commented. It was only a few days ago when it happened, so I could understand Saint's protectiveness. But then again, it seemed all of the MC brothers I'd met through Lucas and Kylo were the same. Though, Saint and Kylo were new to a relationship. Which they'd kept a secret. But I'd found out when I'd met Kylo at a café the day of the incident and told him about my crush on a client and how I needed advice.

I'd left in disbelief, since he'd told me that *straight* Saint, who had a reputation for being a man whore with the ladies, and was Lucas's brother, had come out as bi after Kylo gave him a head job. After I caught my breath from near choking, I told him I wouldn't say anything about them. I was sure Kylo only told me because I'd fucked up. Still, I knew one thing after our chat. I had to end things with Adrik. I wanted what Kylo had found in Saint.

His one.

Smiling, which was a little shaky, I made my way over to the bed, bent, and gently hugged Kylo. "I'm so glad you're okay."

"Thanks."

"All right, that's enough," Saint clipped.

Kylo snorted. "Saint, don't you have to get goin'?"

He glanced at the clock on the wall. "Fuck, I do." He leaned down and kissed Kylo. You would have thought it would have been chaste since there was another person in the room. But no. I had to turn away before I got a semi. My dick was tired of my hand.

"Later, West, and tell my brother when he gets here, he's a dickhead."

"Runs in the family," Kylo called, causing Saint to laugh.

Moving around the bed, I pulled the seat close and sat down. I hated seeing Kylo like this. I hated what happened to him. But I knew, with the smile on his face, that with Saint's help, he would be okay.

"Hey," Kylo called, and I looked up. "How you doin'?"

Shaking my head, I laughed. "It's me who should be asking you that."

His jaw clenched. "I'll be fine as soon as the cunt is found."

"No news yet?"

"Nothin', but the brothers will get him."

I nodded. "I know they will."

"You seen that guy?"

Biting down on my bottom lip, I shook my head. "No."

"He'll come around."

I snorted. "I don't think so."

"You told Lucas yet?"

"Not yet, but I will."

"Told me what?" I jumped at Lucas's voice from the doorway.

"Um… well…." I didn't want to bring it up now.

Lucas made his way over, hugged Kylo, and took a seat opposite me, just as Kylo said, "West has a couple of days before his lease is up, and he needs to move out."

I glared at Kylo. The conniving shithead just threw me under the bus, even though he was right.

I waved it off with a laugh. "It's fine. I'm just going to stay in a motel until I find a new place."

Lucas shook his head. "No you won't."

Hell.

"Lucas, you and Wreck haven't been in there long. I'm not—"

His hand shot up, and Kylo chuckled but then wheezed and held an arm across his ribs. Served him right. Only I regretted that thought as soon as I had it. Kylo didn't deserve anything; he was only trying to look out for me.

Lucas ordered, "You'll move in with us. No ifs, buts, or any other bullpoop."

Suddenly, I wanted to cry. I clenched my jaw, sniffed, and stared down at the white hospital sheets.

"West?" Lucas said gently.

Sucking in a shuddering breath, I told them, "My life before college wasn't easy." I looked up and smiled sadly at Lucas. "I know I haven't said much about my parents, and you might think they're supportive, but they aren't. If I didn't have the scholarship, they would have me still living under their roof and rules." I rubbed my sweaty hands down my jean-clad thighs. "They don't know I'm gay. They believe it's a sin. They're very religious and controlling. They refuse to help me with rent or food because they think it's foolish to move away from them. They said I could have gone to a college close to them, and they would have helped with everything because I would still be living with them. But I couldn't. I had to get out. I had to live, and breathe, and be myself."

"Of course you did," Lucas said. He knew how lucky he was with his parents. They were amazing and loved Lucas and Saint so much, no matter what. Even Kylo lucked out with his parents—his foster ones—Boom and Wendy.

"I don't hate my parents. But I do resent them shoving religion down my throat and having me thinking there was something wrong with me for being gay."

"I'm fuckin' glad you got out," Kylo stated.

I nodded. "Me too, and I guess I'm telling you both this because I wanted to say thank you." Smiling, I looked at them both. "Thank you for caring and wanting to help."

Lucas sniffed and wiped at his eyes. "We always will."

"Fuck yeah," Kylo said.

And now I had that off my chest, I needed the subject moved on before I felt too awkward for sharing.

"So," Lucas drew out. "Does this mean you'll listen and move in with us?"

Grinning, I replied, "Yes. It'll just be for a while—"

He clicked his fingers to shut me up. "I don't care how long. We'd be happy to have you."

Kylo and I snorted. We knew Lucas would be happy about it, but Wreck wouldn't. However, the guy wouldn't say anything. He'd go along with whatever made Lucas happy.

"Wade won't care."

Kylo and I chuckled, which ended with Kylo groaning.

"He won't," Lucas demanded.

"Sure," Kylo said and patted his arm. "Shit, I completely forgot," Kylo stated, looking at me. "Since both of us haven't been comfortable working at Polished, I spoke to Death about some jobs in surveillance for his security company, and he's looking into it for us."

"That sounds great. I've been worried that if any professors or doctors found out I worked at Polished, my career would be down the drain before it even started."

"Speaking of. You two need to scat. I love you visiting, but you both need to study, and I need some beauty sleep, or I'll never heal and perform for Saint."

Lucas screwed up his face and covered his ears with his hands. "That's my cue to go. Besides, we have to get West moved in."

"We what?" was roughly snarled from the doorway.

Lucas was up out of his seat and across the room in seconds. He wrapped his arms around Wreck and beamed up at him. "We have a new roommate. Isn't it wonderful? West is staying with us for however long he wants while we finish our studies."

Wreck's jaw clenched, and his eyes lasered across the room to both Kylo and me before he looked back down at Lucas, who was still smiling. "Great," he grumbled.

A bang on my bedroom door had me jumping and screaming. It opened, and in it stood Lucas's man, Wreck. "Dinner."

I glared, then stretched from leaning over a medical text-book. "You scared the crap out of me, Wreck."

His stare reminded me of Adrik. Like a lot of things did.

"Dinner," Wreck stated again.

"I was just going to grab something later—"

"Now," he bit out before he turned and stomped away. He was a big, scary, but good-looking guy. It still surprised me that my best friend, who was trim, short, and bubbly, had won him over. Even managed to turn a straight guy his way. Seriously, it was something I'd only heard about in books. But Wreck was walking proof that it could happen.

I placed the textbook aside. For my own safety, I'd listen to Wreck and go and eat dinner. I'd only been living with them for a couple of days, and it felt more like home than any other place had. Even when I lived with my parents. It had a lot to do with Lucas.

"West," the man cheered as I walked into the dining room. "We need to keep our strength up while we study. How about later we bring our books out here and do it together?"

"Do what together?" Wreck clipped, coming from the kitchen with three bottles of beer.

Lucas rolled his eyes but smiled up at his man. "Study." He glanced back to me.

I nodded, taking a bite of the pasta in front of me. "Sounds good," I said around a mouthful. I hadn't realized I was so hungry. "Have you heard from Kylo or Saint? I texted Kylo before but haven't got a response yet."

He nodded. "I spoke to Saint, and he said Kylo's been resting a lot. I still can't believe what happened to Kylo. Thank God he's okay."

My stomach twisted. "I know, same."

"But I also can't believe that *my* brother is dating a guy," Lucas said.

"I know," I drew out, and then winced when they both stared at me.

"You knew before the hospital?" Lucas accused.

"Um—"

"You did. When, how, why didn't you say anything?"

Wreck raised a brow at me, and I had a feeling if I didn't give his man my answers in seconds, to stop the hurt look on his face, I was about to be hurt myself.

"I only found out that day," I rushed out. "I met him at a café to talk, and he told me—"

"Why wasn't I invited?" he demanded.

Wreck's fisted hands dropped to the table, and he scooted his chair back a little.

I near pissed myself. "Because I was depressed, and I didn't want to dump my shit on you and your happy little bubble with Wreck."

"Are you serious?" Lucas snapped.

Wreck stood, my eyes widened, and I looked behind me to make sure the area was clear for me to run.

"Wade," Lucas called. Only Lucas could call Wreck by his real name, since they were practically married to one another. Lucas circled his hand around Wreck's wrist. Well, not all the way around, since his partner was a big, scary bastard. I adored the guy deep down, though, because he treated my friend like Lucas was Bella to his Edward. "Sit down. You're scaring him." Wreck sat while Lucas carried on speaking. "And it'll be me who beats him for being the worst friend in the universe." Wreck pulled his chair in, smirking. Lucas clicked his fingers in front of me, and as soon as I looked back at him, he said, "You can talk to me at any time for anything, no matter how happy I am."

"I know, I'm sorry. I... I don't know what I was thinking. I should have included you, but I'm confused, and..." I glanced at Wreck and then away, down to my plate of pasta.

"I'm already putting you both out enough with moving in here." I shrugged, then cried out, "Ouch, Jesus." I moved back to rub my shin where Lucas had kicked. "What did you do that for?"

"You're not putting us out," he bit out. "Like I've said, the house is huge. There's enough room for the three of us."

I nodded.

Wreck stood, then bent to kiss Lucas quickly before picking up his plate. "I'm not leaving because of you. Get shit off your chest by telling Lucas," Wreck ordered and walked out of the room.

Lucas watched him and sighed lovingly with a small smile on his lips. He faced me again and frowned. "Did I do something that said you couldn't come to me?"

"No!" I swiped a hand at the back of my neck. "I honestly just thought that I didn't want to burden you with anything because you're so happy."

"Well, now you know I want to know and that I will always be here for you no matter the moment. Spill."

"Okay." I nodded, pushing the plate away.

Lucas's lips pinched. "You didn't eat enough."

"I'm not hungry." The thought of the conversation we were about to have had taken away the hunger I'd felt.

Lucas glared. "I'll make you something later when we study."

"Deal." Leaning back in the seat, I started, "A main reason I went to Kylo, and only him, was because I hoped he would be in the same situation as I was in." I gave him a sad smile. "I fucked up with work."

Lucas's brows dipped, and he cocked his head to the side. "What do you mean?"

I grabbed the bottle of beer and took a long drink from it before I rested it back on the table and crossed my arms over my chest. In a way, I wanted to tell Lucas, as I didn't want to hide it from him, but I still felt like a fool for catching feelings.

"West, are you okay?" Lucas asked softly.

Lifting my gaze, I nodded. "Yeah, yes… I'm a mess because I'm an idiot. I did the one thing I shouldn't have and got feelings for a client. Adrik… he's…" I smiled to myself, but then shook my head. "…grumpy, curt, but nice, sweet, handsome. He also has a Russian accent. Nothing I expected on my first job." I shrugged. "Maybe that was it… him being my first client, but from the first meeting, I couldn't get him out of my mind. Seriously, I thought about him all the time." I leaned forward. "Lucas, we haven't even kissed, and I turned into a lovesick puppy over the man."

"Did he… are you and him…?"

"Nothing. We're nothing because I ended it after only seeing him a few times. I ended the gig because I had to protect my heart and knew he wouldn't want me for anything more than my time to keep him company." I grazed my top teeth over my bottom lip. "He seemed lonely, Lucas. So lonely, and maybe that was another reason I was stuck on him. We matched. Before meeting you, and now Kylo, I didn't have anyone I could call a friend. Yes, we had the others we caught up with through college, but to me, they were only acquaintances."

"I agree," he said.

"I had to end things."

"It sounds like you made the right choice."

"Then why do I feel like running back to his place and seeing him?"

Lucas smiled sadly. "You miss him."

It wasn't a question, but I nodded anyway. Shaking my head, I moved on. "Anyway, it was when I spoke to Kylo about what I should do about the client, when he blurted out about Saint. I was sure it was to make me feel better." I chuckled halfheartedly. Thinking of Adrik had my mind locking on to him, and even then, I wanted to see him.

I missed him, which made no sense since I hardly knew him.

"How about we go get our books, and while we study, you can eat one of those chocolate muffins I made."

"Sounds like a plan." I smiled, but I knew it didn't reach my eyes. I felt too twisty on the inside for anything real. It was ridiculous and something a teenager would be like after a breakup. I hadn't broken up with anyone, really, so I was acting this way for nothing. I had to stop.

I had to.

CHAPTER SEVEN
ADRIK

Six long and fucking tiring weeks, and I still hadn't gone after who I wanted. I blamed work, parents, but also the fact how he seemed happy. I could tell from the photographic proof sitting on my desk on my kitchen counter in front of me. I had lost count of the times I brought these out to look at. Like some stalker. Except, even when I tried to throw them away after seeing his smile, witnessing his happiness, I couldn't bring myself to do it.

My not seeking him out had nothing to do with the concern of rejection.

"Motherfucking stubborn ass," I mumbled to myself in Russian. I was weak, too worried he would not want me. I worried where I should have been taking control and seeing him, telling him I wanted him in my life.

I picked an image up and brought it closer. It was of West leaving Polished with security following him, but he'd stopped near his car and looked off in the distance, as if seeing someone he knew.

Then another when he moved into a new house. Dimitri found out it was with his friend Lucas and his partner, Wreck, who was a part of the Diamond Motorcycle Club. I did not like seeing him laughing with another, but at least I knew they were only friends.

The most recent was of West walking from the college campus. The wind had made his hair fall into his eyes; his hand was up about to brush it away.

I missed him.

His smile, his eyes, his mouth as he spoke too much, but enough that I enjoyed seeing what would come from him.

Had I left it too long?

Did he have someone else?

He still worked at the escort agency. I clenched my jaw when my gaze landed on him out on a date with a client. A man old enough to be his father. I hated those photos the most. It seared my insides to a point I thought I would burn from the inside out.

Was he actually happy?

Did he care that he hadn't seen me?

I knew nothing of his thoughts, but I wanted to.

Soon. I needed answers, and I was now impatient to get them. As soon as my parents were out of the States, I would approach West and see where things would go.

It had been good having my parents around, but they had stayed too long. I had thought Papa would want to get back for business, but something kept them here.

I lifted my head when I heard footsteps approach. Quickly, I moved the photos into one pile and managed to get them into the drawer just as my mother walked around the corner with Papa following.

"I thought I was meeting you downstairs for lunch?" I asked in Russian.

"We need to speak," Papa replied.

Tensing, I nodded toward the table. Had my parents seen the photos? I moved around the counter, glancing back to make sure the drawer was closed. It was. After Mama sat, I took the chair opposite her while Papa took the head of the table.

"What is wrong?"

"You," Papa barked in English.

"What about me?"

Mama rested a hand on Papa's arm. *"My boy, we have been here a long time now, and you've kept us busy seeing sights, which we have loved. But we worry about you since all we see is you working. No dates. No life."*

"Mama, I'm not interested in them."

"Is it too much running three casinos and the bars?" Papa asked.

"No."

"It's not only that," Mama stated, back in English. It was no wonder I switched languages so much when Mama always did. Papa nodded and sat back, letting Mama lead. *"We notice a sadness in you, my boy. A sadness only a person can put there. Was there someone who broke your heart?"*

"*I will kill them,*" Papa clipped, banging the table with his fist.

Leaning forward, I placed my elbows on the table and rubbed a hand over my face. "*I am fine. There is nothing to worry about.*"

"So there isn't anyone?"

"*No.*"

My phone, thankfully, picked that moment to ring. I held up a finger and took it out of my pocket. When I saw Leonid's name, I said, "I have to take this."

"Of course," Mama replied.

"Da?"

"The guard Ben had is here. He needs to speak with you."

My gut dropped. Something has happened. "Send him up," I ordered, and then hung up, only to press in another number and place it back to my ear as I stood and started pacing.

"*Dimitri, where is he?*"

"*I was about to call you. We don't know.*"

My blood seized in my veins. "*What do you mean?*" I snarled.

"*I had Pavel on West at college. When he didn't call in, I rang him, but there was no answer.*" He took a breath. "*Fuck, Adrik, I'm here now. Pavel was knocked out; looks like a drug was used because I see no wound. He hasn't woken in the time I got here. How did you know something had happened?*"

"*The guard from his work is here. I'll call you back. Check his car is there.*"

"*I will.*"

"Adrik, what is it?" Papa asked as soon as I hung up.

"Wait, please," I said, and made my way out to the elevator. I knew my parents were following, but I had no care what they heard. I only needed information on what was going on.

I stepped around the corner as the doors slid open.

"Is Ben here?" the man demanded.

"*West* is not here—"

"How do you know his fuckin' name?" He stepped off the elevator.

I pulled the gun from my back holster and raised it. "Do not move again. I know his name like you probably know things about me. Research. Tell me what you know of his whereabouts and also your name."

"Death."

"Death? What is this?" Papa called.

"My name." He didn't look away from me as he spoke. "West's friend said he should be home, but he's not. He got worried when West didn't answer his phone. I was in the area. I had to check if he was here."

"Why would he be here?"

Death glared. "A hunch."

I lowered my gun and put it away. "I had a man on him, but that man is unconscious. West was taken from college."

"Jesus motherfuckin' Christ," he bellowed and pulled his phone from his pocket. With jerky movements, he then put it to his ear. "Wreck, he's not here. Hail had a man on him…. I don't fuckin' know why…. Yeah, said the guy's unconscious, and West was taken from college. Get the brothers on it—"

"I have a man at the college. He will help—"

"We don't need your help."

"He *will* be fucking helping whether you like it or not."

"Fuck! You get that? Yeah…." To me, he asked, "What's the guy's name?"

"Dimitri."

"It's Dimitri. All right, I'll be there soon. Yeah, of course. Stay with Lucas. Shit, you better call Saint. He can tell Gun. Okay," he clipped and then hung up. He glanced to the panel and pressed the button. The doors opened.

"I am coming with you," I demanded.

"No, you ain't. I'm not goin' to the scene, but to his house to—"

"I either come or I go on my own but believe me, I will find information in any way I can."

"Fucking hell, fine. Then I can keep an eye on you."

I started for the elevator when Mama called, "Adrik?"

Stopping, I glanced back to see her holding Papa's arm, frowning. "Wait in the lobby," I ordered Death.

Death glanced from me over my shoulder and back again. He sighed. "Hurry." The doors closed, and I heard the elevator leave the floor.

I faced my parents. *"I'm sorry I won't be attending lunch."*

"We figured, son. What's going on. Do you need me to come? To call more men in?"

"No. I will handle it. Someone I know has been taken, and we need to find him."

"Is it someone you care for? A man?" Mama asked gently.

My heart doubled its beat. Sweat beaded at the back of my neck. Still, I said, *"Yes. A man, a good man who I care for."*

Mama smiled. I looked at my father. He seemed tense, but he nodded. *"Then go."*

"Papa—"

He shook his head and stepped in front of me, where he cupped the side of my neck. *"The Mikhaillova family is ruthless and cruel, but we love one another fiercely. No matter what, son, I will always love you. Find this man so we can meet the person who has captured my son's heart."*

I found it hard to breathe as I stared into my father's unwavering gaze. He meant it. Every word. He would support me, love me, even when I wanted to be with a man. Dimitri had been right. I was a fool thinking otherwise.

"I love you."

He pounded his chest with his fist. *"You'll always have my heart."* He gently pushed me back. "Now go."

I nodded, glancing over my father's shoulder. *"Mama, I love you."*

Tears brimmed her eyes, her hands clasped in front of her. *"I love you, my boy. Through everything. Call us if you need anything."*

"Da, anything," Papa stated with a nod before he turned and collected Mama under his arm. *"Come, my precious, we will have lunch in our place and wait for our son to call."*

How could I be happy and filled with dread all at the same time? No matter, all I knew was that I had to find West.

KYLO

"Where the fuck is he? And where in the motherfuck are you taking me?" I demanded harshly to my man.

His hand on my thigh tightened. "We're going to Lucas. You can help him. Wreck and I'll head out to help the other brothers."

"You are not keeping me fuckin' locked away like some soft bitch."

"Kylo, babe, please. You know me better than that. I'd have you at my side, but what about Lucas? My brother, your friend? He's out of his mind crazy right now, and since you're both close friends to West, it'll be better having you at his side than me or even Wreck."

I shook my head. "That's bullshit."

"I'm not fuckin' with you. Just take a damn breath and think about it."

With my hands fisted, I pressed them into my eyes and breathed. Fear, all I could feel was fear. Lucas would be feeling the same. The others didn't know West, hadn't connected with West like we had.

Dropping my hands, I sighed. "You're right. I'll stay with Lucas."

He picked up my hand and kissed the back of it while he parked out the front of Lucas and Wreck's place. "Love you," he said.

Still, my heart fluttered from hearing it. "Love you too."

I grabbed my walking stick as we climbed out of the car, and before we reached the front door, it opened. Lucas's hands covered his stomach, his brows pinched, and his eyes sad. "Have you heard anything new?" he asked.

"Nothin'," I said, reaching him and bringing him into my arms. "We'll find him."

He nodded into my chest.

Wreck appeared behind us. His hands dropped to Lucas's waist. "Babe, come back inside. You don't have any shoes on, and it's cold."

Lucas turned into Wreck, who moved him inside, and we both followed. In the living room, Lucas sat curled into Wreck on the couch. I took an armchair while Saint sat on the arm of it with his hand on my shoulder.

"Maybe he's out with other friends?" Saint suggested.

Lucas and I shook our heads. "We're his only friends."

"A date?" Wreck said.

"No, he would have told us," Lucas replied. He sucked in his bottom lip and bit down. "What happened if a client… if they liked him too much and kidnapped him?"

"Death checks all backgrounds. He knows what to look for. It won't be one of them," Saint said.

"Can you be completely sure?" I asked.

Saint and Wreck shared a look. Wreck sighed. "Death was at the only one we weren't sure about." He shook his head. "He'd been looking out for West, had a man on him, but that man is unconscious at the college."

"Who was the client, and why would he have someone watching West?" Lucas demanded before I could.

"Adrik Hail," Wreck clipped.

I shared a look with Lucas. Adrik was the man West had

feelings for. Had it been reciprocated this whole time? Fuck, it must have been if he had a guard on West.

I stood. "Then we need to go talk to him. He might have more information."

"Not needed. That's all the information he had—"

"But—"

There was a knock on the door before it opened, and Death strode in. Someone else followed. A guy I didn't know.

"What the fuck is he doin' here?" Wreck demanded, standing.

"Who is he?" Lucas asked, joining Wreck.

Death glared at the man beside him. "He wouldn't take no for an answer. I thought it better I bring him, so he didn't get anyone we know in trouble."

"Why are there cars pulling up outside?" Saint asked. I hadn't noticed he'd walked over to the window.

"They are my men."

I spun my gaze back to the man with a Russian accent. Adrik Hail. And from Lucas's gasp, he'd worked out who he was as well.

"You're Adrik," Lucas blurted.

Adrik's cold gaze fell on Lucas. "Da."

"Just found out his father's Nicholai Mikhaillova," Death announced.

Wreck was the only one who obviously knew the name. "Get the fuck outta my house."

"Nyet, I am here to help. I *will* help."

Wreck started for him but froze when Adrik swiftly pulled

a gun and pointed it at him. "You will not stop me from helping."

"Fuck, I shoulda taken the damn gun off you," Death commented with a groan.

"Wade," Lucas said softly. He stepped up and curled his hands around Wreck's arm. "Let's calm down a second and find out more information."

"Yeah, like why Wreck had a freak-out over his father's name," I said, leaning into my cane. "Because I don't have a fuckin' clue, and I want to move this shit along so we can find West."

"Da, I agree." Adrik put his gun away. "My father runs the Russian mafia *in* Russia. I am no part of the mafia. I own businesses, and that is all. Nonetheless, I have killed and will kill for the people I care for."

Of fucking course he just had to add that, which had Wreck growling under his breath.

Saint stepped forward, obviously sensing my lessening patience. "Right, so your dad's the mafia, but none of it will touch us or the ones we care about."

"Da."

"I'm guessin' that means yes?"

Adrik nodded.

"Okay, let's join forces and move on. We all want the same thing. West home and safe."

Everyone stayed silent for a moment.

"My men called from the college," Adrik said. "They are with your men," he said to Death, meaning our brothers. "West's vehicle was found. Nothing was missing or broken."

I shook my head, thinking. "He couldn't just have been abducted in broad daylight without people noticing."

Death cleared his throat. "Tech got a hold of the cameras. It caught West walkin' outta the building, but the way he went to the parking lot didn't have a camera angle."

"Did he seem different? Scared? Agitated? Anything?" Lucas asked.

Death shook his head. "Tech said he looked fine. But he did mention he must have seen something off camera, the way West ended up going. He seemed shocked but then smiled as if—"

"He recognized someone," I said.

"Exactly." Death nodded.

"So it's someone he knows," Lucas commented.

"How about you three stay here and keep thinking, while Wreck, Death, and I get out there to help the others?" Saint suggested.

"You want me to stay here?" Adrik said with a sneer. "I have more men than your club has. I will go out there and look—"

"Saint's right," I told him. "You could help us here. I'm sure there are people you could call. Clubs, casinos, put out a description in case he's out with someone he knew partying and just forgot about us."

"He wouldn't," Lucas whispered.

Wreck wrapped an arm around Lucas's chest. "It's worth a try, right?"

Lucas sighed but nodded.

"What do you say?" I asked Adrik.

"Fine. I will speak with my men, leave half here, the rest will follow. They will take orders from you," he said to Death. Adrik turned and walked out of the house to speak with his men.

"Got it. Let's hit the road." Death started for the door. Saint stepped in front of me, and I could see Wreck saying goodbye to Lucas.

"Be fuckin' safe, you ass," I told him.

Saint chuckled, leaned in, and kissed my nose, then mouth. "You know I will. Can't have you missin' me."

"Damn right."

"Fuck me, I need to get a woman," Death grumbled. "Come the fuck on," he bit out before he left.

Saint and Wreck walked out after a final kiss, and Lucas and I moved over to the window.

"He cares," Lucas said. "A lot."

I nodded, knowing he was talking about Adrik. "He does. We need West back to see it."

"We do."

Fuck, I hoped wherever he was, he was okay.

CHAPTER EIGHT
WEST

EARLIER

alking from my final class for the day, I couldn't help but smile. It was only days until exams, and I felt good about them. I'd studied hard and knew the information. Now it just had to stick with me on the day.

"West" was called. I glanced up and over to the right. My eyes widened, and shock settled in. I forced a smile at them and started toward my parents. Closer, I called, "Mom, Dad, what are you doing here?"

"We haven't seen you in a while. We thought lunch would be nice," Mom said without a smile, like usual.

"Um, I think… I mean—"

"Stop blabbering, stand up straight, and answer your mother," Dad ordered.

Like always when he used that stern tone, I knew to listen.

With gritted teeth at my weakness for not standing up for myself, I straightened my shoulders and replied, "Lunch would be good." Then they could leave, and it would be another few months before I saw them again. If I did. Maybe this day would be the one I stood up for myself and told them I was gay. They'd disown me, but I couldn't find it in me to care. I had my own little family with Lucas and Kylo. They cared. The people in front of me didn't.

"I'll follow you, if you have a place in mind," I said.

"No. You'll come in our car, and we'll drop you off after," Dad stated.

I breathed out a frustrated breath through my nose. "Of course."

Mom turned. "This way."

As soon as my dad followed her, I slouched, stuck up my middle finger, and regrettably went after them. One day I would stop acting like a scared child who got scolded over the littlest things and stand up for myself.

Today just could be the day, because I knew I didn't want to see them again, even in this small amount of time. I'd grown. I was happy, to an extent, and had a life. I didn't want them to tarnish it by their bullshit.

"You may sit up front," Mom said at the car, which had me stilling. She never let me before, why now? Suspicion dipped my brows. However, I was probably being an idiot. Maybe they were trying to change.

"Thank you." I smiled and slipped into the seat that Dad held the door open to. He closed it and walked around the front to the driver side. I wanted to be anywhere but here.

Shit, I'd even take a dentist visit or a waxing over being there.

Dad started the car and backed out of the space while I strapped my belt in. "There's a nice restaurant not far from here. I could give you directions," I suggested, since they'd never come to visit me before.

"I don't need it," Dad replied. He gripped the steering wheel. "You didn't call your mother for the monthly check-in."

Shit. I hadn't even realized it had passed.

"I'm sorry. Study and work have kept me busy."

Dad grunted.

"We were worried," Mom said from the seat behind me.

"I really am sorry. I promise it won't happen again." I could have slapped my own forehead for forgetting. I should have known they would come to see me when I didn't check in. It was my own damn fault they were there, and now I wanted to kick myself as well.

"You've been a bad boy, West," Dad said.

I laughed. "What?"

"Do not laugh," Dad bellowed. His hands kept gripping and releasing the wheel over and over again.

Shit, he was beyond pissed.

"It was one time I missed," I said, suddenly annoyed.

His upper lip raised, he sneered. "I'm not talking about that."

Fuck. "W-What are you talking about?"

Dad said nothing; instead, Mom did. "Your father and I have been in town for a while, West."

I stilled. My stomach churned, and I wanted to throw up. "Really?" I managed to get out through a breath.

Mom hummed, then said, "Yes. We have witnessed a lot."

Bile raced up my throat. I cleared it and swallowed thickly. "Like what?"

"Your sins," Dad snarled.

No!

"It's time for you to be cleansed, West," Mom said.

A sharp pain touched my neck. I tried to turn, but Dad's hand shot out to hold my head in place.

"What are you doing?" I slurred. My limbs, I couldn't lift them. I couldn't fight. Terror filled me as fatigue like I hadn't experienced before washed over me. "W-What's happening?"

"We're going to purge your sins out of you, West" was the last thing I heard before sleep dragged me under.

Groaning, I went to roll over but realized I couldn't. My body ached and my knees hurt. I shivered from the frigid air, and a headache pounded in my head.

Had I been out drinking?

I blinked again and again. Slowly, I lifted my head, waiting for my eyes to focus. When they did, I gasped.

"No, no, no, no." I was naked.

Naked.

I reared back, only to cry out and fall forward. Chains rattled, tears blurring my vision, but I still saw and felt them.

Cold steel wrapped around my wrists, the chains bolted to the ground, keeping me in place.

"Please, please, no," I begged the silent room.

I glanced around at the shelves, the food on them, the bench next to it, the only light shining down in the dingy, cold room.

Why?

Why the fuck was I chained naked in my parents' basement?

A basement I had always been scared of because my father used to lock me down here when I'd done something wrong. He made me read from the bible over and over until my throat hurt.

"Mom? Dad?" I yelled. Anger filled me, warmed me. They'd gone too far. Way too fucking far. They were crazy. I didn't want anything to do with them. Never again.

I heard footsteps. A door opened and closed before the one to the basement opened. More pounding footsteps down the stairs. I tried to glance over my shoulder, but I couldn't see who it was.

I rattled the chains. "You're nuts. This is fucking crazy. Let me go," I yelled.

"You will be cleansed," Dad replied, almost robotically.

"What are you talking about? Is this because of my job? I don't do anything with those men."

"Lies," he screamed. "You let them touch you."

"I didn't!"

"You did. It's wrong. You're wrong. We can't have that.

God won't allow something like you in Heaven until your sins are purged from you."

"What are you talking about? Working isn't a sin. Being gay isn't a sin. You're the one who's wrong. I'm not. I'm normal. I'm fine the way I am."

"You repulse us. *We* will make you clean" came Mom's voice. I hadn't heard her approach. She moved beside me as she placed a tray on the bench.

"Mom, no, what are you talking about? Please, please stop this." My voice cracked, tears welling.

I wasn't wrong.

I wasn't a sin.

My actions weren't sins.

I just wanted to be accepted. I wanted a happy life—one filled with love.

I was normal. I was.

"Stop, *please*. There's nothing wrong with me. There isn't." A sob tore out of me. I thumped the ground with the chains. "I'm normal. I am!"

My heart cracked. It dripped blood from an old wound. One my parents had inflicted. One I had healed by being away from them, but it was the same one they were opening again. They were breaking me.

"You will be clean. You will be after we're done with you," Mom stated.

I glanced up to a mother who never loved me—a mother who only saw faults.

"Don't do this, please, Mom. *Please*."

Her upper lip raised in a silent snarl as she watched my

tears flow down my cheeks. "You're dirty, boy. God won't have you the way you are."

"He will!" I yelled. I believed it. I may not be devoted, but I trusted God existed. "He will have me. He will shine down on me. He will love me for who I am. But can you really say this is what God would want you to do to your own son? Doesn't what you're doing go against God and his ways?"

She shook her head and glanced over me. "God doesn't shine on those who sin."

"What you're doing is a sin!" I shouted.

"You're wrong. God trusted in *us* to take care of *our* problem. I am doing God's work, and you will repent. Hold him."

My head was forced back with a hand in my hair and one under my chin. I shook my head over and over, moved, wiggled. Dad gripped my hair harder, nearly ripping it from my scalp.

"Still," he ordered.

Mom turned back from the bench with a jug in her hand. "Vinegar is a good tool to cleanse with."

Vinegar.

She didn't. She couldn't want to pour that down my throat.

"Open," she said.

I shook my head, clamping my lips closed. More tears fell. My whimpers came thick and fast as I pulled on the chains, skin scraping against the cold metal.

Dad shook my head violently by my hair. "Do what she says."

Still, I fought. I pulled, tried to slide my legs back to kick him, but he stepped down on my feet. I sobbed, cried. Pain raced through me—so much pain over my body.

Mom reached forward with one hand and pinched my cheeks together while Dad dropped his grip on my throat to pinch my nose. My eyes widened, a dull whine rasping out of my tender throat.

I needed to breathe. I needed air.

The crack in my heart grew wider as I opened my mouth wide and gasped for oxygen. In an instant, the liquid, acidic and raw, gushed down my throat. I choked, coughed, and fought for another breath, but they wouldn't stop. It kept coming.

It burned. My throat lit with a flame I'd never felt.

My eyes welled for a different reason.

Their hands dropped away, and I fell forward, choking, coughing, spitting, gasping, crying. My stomach rebelled and I vomited. More burning followed.

It hurt.

It hurt so much.

I didn't deserve *this*. I didn't. I hadn't done anything other than want to be myself and want love like my friends had.

I wasn't a bad person.

Through a shuddering breath, I rasped, "You'll pay." The words stabbed my fiery throat, but it was worth it for the look of shock on my mother's face.

She blanked her features and shook her head. "Lies are a sin, boy. You know this. We taught you this. Do you see?" she screamed. "Do you see how the time away from us has corrupted you?"

I chuckled, pushing aside the hurt. "Always been gay," I managed to get out.

"Force him to stay down." Mom walked back over to the bench.

I could take whatever they delivered to live another day, to find what I wanted in life. I could survive this and get back to the people who knew me, who loved me.

Dad's grip on me fell away. I tried to roll to the side, but he kicked me in the ribs. Another dry cough raked over me as agony burst to life.

He stopped in front of me, kneeling where my hands were tied. He pulled the chains taut. I tugged back on them, but from the agony, I'd already grown weak.

"Move, and it will be worse," Mom said from my side.

"Stop," I grated.

Dad tsked. "Not until you're cleansed."

They started praying as I felt something sharp dig into the opposite side of my back from where Mom stood leaning over me. The throbbing sting grew across my whole back. I cried out and thrashed, but it didn't stop.

Glancing to the side, I caught the glint of a sharp knife.

She was cutting my skin open.

"Stop, stop, please."

She didn't.

Another slice had me tearing more skin on my wrists as I tried to get away, tried to fight. Still, their voices grew louder with their prayer. It wasn't until my mom reached my lower back that she stepped away.

"We cut the sins away." She moved to the bench, and I

heard the clatter of the knife even over my heavy breaths and sobs. "We cleanse through the wounds, purging you for the evil deeds you have done."

She turned with another jug in her hands.

"No, no, no," I whimpered. I thrashed and screamed, but nothing I did helped. Nothing.

Shaking my head, I begged over and over, but she didn't stop. She tipped the jug's contents over my back.

I roared as my skin sizzled. There was nothing but blistering agony until the blackness took me.

Only I wasn't gone long. I woke screaming when a new scorching heat touched my back.

"He's awake," I heard Mom say.

A foot to my ribs rocked me to the side, and I blinked through the tears to see Dad standing there holding a bright red, burning branding iron with a cross on it.

I curled into myself whimpering, crying, realizing he'd just seared it into my skin.

"You will be cleansed after we repeat this every night for a week," Mom said.

I shook my head.

Mom crouched beside me. "This is good for you, West. God will see the lengths you've gone to be admitted into Heaven. He will welcome you with open arms. We're doing this for you."

"F-Fuck you," I managed through what felt like a throat full of razor blades.

"Respect your mother," Dad yelled.

"Fuck you too."

"Harold, leave him. We knew it would take time after the evil things he's done." With that, they walked out of the room and left me in agony on the dirty floor. Their son.

No. I wasn't their son. They weren't my parents. They never would be again.

I wasn't evil. I was a fucking human being who had been put through hell. I couldn't move, couldn't lift my head. I couldn't do anything but breathe and cry through the pain.

Please, God, if you're listening, help me or take me away from here. Please.

This is fucking useless," I snarled, throwing my phone to the table. Leaning forward, I rested my head in my hands.

"We have to keep trying," Lucas said softly.

Lifting my head, I nodded as Kylo placed a mug of coffee in front of me. "Blagodaryu vas."

"If that was thank you, you're welcome," Kylo said around a yawn.

I nodded as Lucas said, "It is." We both stared at him. He shrugged. "I know a little from an online class a couple of years ago."

Kylo snorted. "Means he knows a lot with that big brain of his."

"Eto tak?" I asked.

Lucas rolled his eyes. "Nyet. It's not right. My brain isn't that big."

It was good Lucas knew some, because exhaustion had me

switching between English and Russian, but all of us were tired, having not been to sleep, and it was now early hours the next morning.

The next morning, and we still had not heard anything. Pavel, the man I had on West, was still unconscious from the drug. No matter what happened, his excuse would not be enough. For his mistake, he would be taught a lesson so it would never happen again.

No one had a clue what had happened.

Meaning no one knew where West was.

I did not like it. My chest ached, and I rubbed at it for the millionth time as worry warred behind my ribs. My gut twisted, and I could not stop thinking the worst. Not knowing ate at me, and I was ready to fight something, anything.

"What about if we *did* try his parents?" Lucas suggested. I had mentioned them a while ago, but they both waved it off, saying that West did not really speak with them.

"Da." I nodded, happy to move on with something.

"Might as well," Kylo agreed, resting his cane against the table before he sat. From my men, I already knew what had happened to Kylo. "What's their names?" he asked.

"Harold and Grace Millbrook," Lucas said. "I'll look them up." He did and then reached for his phone. "I remember West saying they live over an hour away. This has to be it, since it's the only Millbrook," he commented before saying into the phone. "Hello… sorry to disturb you so early, but I'm a friend of your son, West…. Oh, yes, okay." He pulled the phone away from his ear and stared at it. "I don't like it." He glanced at both of us. "They said West didn't live with them and would prefer not to talk about him."

"Who said this? His mother or father?" I snapped.

"Mother."

Gripping the mug, I said, "I have gotten the… how do you say… vibe from West that he was not close to them. They are strict. But why would they not want to talk about him?"

Kylo sat at the dining table. "Hell, we could have had information on him, and they didn't seem to care." He shook his head. "Who's up for a drive?"

"Da, I am. I want to see these parents."

"I don't like the look in your eyes. Kylo, do you like the look in his eyes?"

"It's kinda scary. We gonna have a problem with you goin'?" Kylo asked.

"Nyet, I will behave. I would just like to meet these parents who do not seem to care."

"Um…," Lucas started. When I looked at him, he winced with a smile. "Can we have your gun?"

I stared. There was no way I would give up my weapon.

Kylo snorted. "That'd be a no."

I drank my coffee and stood. "We will go in my car. I will have men follow."

"Is this a good idea? Should we ring Wade and Zion?"

Kylo waved his friend off and also stood, grabbing his cane. "Later." We moved off toward the front door. "Let them keep doin' what they're doin' because they might find somethin', and if we tell them where we're goin', Wreck will hunt us down to protect you. It'll waste their time."

Lucas nodded. "You're right. Besides, I doubt anything will happen, and I don't need protecting."

I snorted, and Lucas looked up at me as he locked the front door. "You are small, cute, and thin. You need protecting."

He glared. "You make me sound like a darn bunny or something. I can be tough when I want to be."

"It's true," Kylo said. "He took down a brother after the guy punched Wreck. Learnin' things about the body gives him the ability to know weaknesses."

I stared at Lucas some more. He looked like a preteen little boy, but I knew he was as old as West and in some of the same classes as him. I nodded, believing Kylo's words. He had no reason to lie.

Turning, I strode to the cars. Leonid folded out of one. "Sir?"

"We are making a trip, and you will follow. I want the others to stay behind."

"Yes, sir."

Moving over to my vehicle, I unlocked it, knowing Leonid would relay my message to the others.

"Do you need a stepping stool to climb in?" I taunted Lucas, since it seemed easy to do. I also hoped it would get back to his partner. I could use a fight to get the energy under my skin out.

He growled under his breath like a little kitten. "Oh ha, ha, ha. Very funny." He climbed up into the back seat and put his belt on, crossing his arms over his chest.

Once I was in the driver seat, I glanced at him in the rearview mirror as I started the car. "You are no bunny, but a kitten, da?"

He rolled his eyes. "I'll let you have your fun since I know it's you only trying to take your mind off West and also to goad me. You probably want me to tell Wade so he can beat you."

He read me well. I did not like it. "I would win."

He laughed. "No, you wouldn't."

It was my turn to roll my eyes. "Maybe one day we will see."

"If you're gonna stick around in West's life, I wouldn't pick a fight with Wreck. He's a fuckin' powerhouse," Kylo said.

"Give me address," I ordered, and once Kylo uploaded it into the device, I added, "Do you not think coming from a mafia family I know how to fight? I killed a man when I was twelve for hurting my mother."

Kylo nodded. "Didn't say you couldn't fight and kill. Just know we can also."

I grunted, presuming as much. I was just agitated and ready to take it out on others because we were running around like headless chickens. We had better get a lead going to see these people.

"Even if this doesn't pan out, we'll find him," Lucas said softly.

After a few moments of silence, I told them, "I do plan to be in West's life."

Kylo smiled. "Good." And I caught Lucas's small grin in the mirror before he turned to look out the window. The rest of the ride was silent, each of us in our own thoughts. Mine consisted of West, and I knew the others were probably thinking the same.

I pulled up at the small house, stopped the car, and took in what was around. The place was run-down, as were the others around it. The house on the right looked to be unoccupied.

"Do we have a plan?" Lucas asked.

"Da, we go in and find out what their problem is."

"We already know. They're religious, strict, and unloving fuckers," Kylo commented. "But let's hope West has been in contact with them." We climbed out of the car.

"Are you taking your cane?" Lucas asked Kylo, who limped heavily along.

"No, and don't fuckin' tell Saint."

Lucas grazed his bottom lip with his top teeth in worry but said nothing.

When Leonid made a move to get out, I held my hand up to them. They would stay until I called for them. I doubted I would have to if, as I presumed, they were bigoted old people.

The curtain to the left of the door twitched. They were watching. Good. I hoped they got scared with three men walking up to their house. Though, Lucas was not intimidating at all.

"They know we are here," I stated, nodding to the curtain, which just moved again.

Kylo grunted. "At least we know they're home then."

On the porch, it was Lucas who stepped forward and knocked. It did not take long before the door opened a little.

"Yes?" the woman asked.

"Hello, I was speaking to you on the phone about West."

"Like I said, West doesn't live here. He's away at college."

She went to close the door. I stepped in and pushed it back against her. She held strong.

"What are you doing?" she snapped.

"We just want to ask some questions. You have no concern for your son?"

"Adrik," Lucas whispered.

"Nyet, this woman should be concerned when no one has seen him in twenty-four fucking hours. But look at you. You glare up at me without a care."

"I *don't* care, because West doesn't want anything to do with us."

"And why is that?" I demanded.

"What's going on here?" The door opened. I dropped my hold, stepping back. In the doorway stood a fat old man. He crossed his arms over his chest. "Leave this property right now. We don't take kindly to people like you."

"Like who?"

"I think he means foreigners," Lucas said.

"Then you won't like my kind either. Name's Gun. I'm a part of the Diamond MC. Remember it. Because if we don't get some damn answers from you, I'll come back with my brothers. You want that?"

"You can't threaten us," the old man yelled, stepping out onto the porch. "Grace, call the police."

"Da, call them, and then we can get them to ask *you* the questions."

"Harold?"

"Wait," he clipped.

There was something with these two that I did not trust— besides them being scum. Any other person still would have gone for the phone and called for help, so why did they not?

"What do you exactly want to know? We've already told you he doesn't live here. He hasn't for a long time, and if he is missing, as you said, he won't come here." His eye twitched. "What else is there to know?"

"I would like some water," I said. I wanted to get in that house. These people were untrustworthy.

"Go get it elsewhere," the woman said.

"One drink and we will go," I tried.

"No," the fat man replied gruffly.

"When was the last time you spoke to West?" Lucas asked.

"Two months ago."

"I thought you said he doesn't want anything to do with you. Why would he speak to you two months ago?" Kylo questioned, making an excellent point.

There was a pause, then the woman said, "I rang him to try and get him to come and see us. It wasn't us who put distance between us, but him. He didn't listen and refused to come home."

Lies. I would never believe West to act that way. He was the most caring man I knew, and that said a lot when I knew many.

"Thanks for your time," Lucas said. "Adrik, Kylo, we should get going."

"Nyet—"

"Adrik. I'm sure West will show up at home." The look he gave me told me he wanted me to drop this and let them go.

"Fine," I snarled and stepped down off the porch.

"Don't come back, or we *will* call the cops," the father threatened. The weak, pathetic man slammed the door shut, and I heard the lock engage.

As soon as Lucas stepped off the porch, I was in his face. I threw out an arm. "What was that? They hide something. I know it."

"They're not going to let us waltz in there. We need a different plan."

"I kill them," I bit out.

Lucas swallowed, his eyes widening. "Well, not yet, until we know what they know."

Crossing my arms over my chest, I barked, "What we do then?"

"We keep an eye on them," Kylo suggested. "Wait until they've gone out and then we'll get in there."

I shook my head. "We do not have time. I want answers now."

A phone rang. Lucas shifted back and pulled his out. His eyes widened. "It's Wade."

"Answer it," Kylo said as I looked back to the house. The curtain moved again.

Lucas squeaked. "Do I lie or tell them where we are? I'm not good at lying."

Kylo snorted. "We know. You can tell them since we'll be here a while now."

"Good, okay…. Hey, Wade, what are you doing?"

"He sounds guilty. He would never be good with torture." I glared at Lucas, who gave me the finger. Any other would piss themselves before they acted such a way with me. He did have balls, after all, but Wade must be his weakness. It was understandable. I could see the love they held for one another.

"No, Adrik didn't say torture."

"But I did."

Kylo chuckled beside us. I crossed my arms over my chest and shifted my gaze back to the house. I half listened to Lucas explain what we were doing while I ran my eyes over the house.

"Shut it," I demanded on a growl.

"What?" Lucas snapped.

I covered his mouth with my hand. "Listen." I was sure I heard something out of place. There were no birds, no neighbors, so what was it?

My eyes widened when I heard it again.

Screams. I looked down and saw a tiny window for a basement. "There." I pointed. I took a step forward when the screaming got louder. "They have him," I snarled, racing for the front door.

WEST

Whimpering woke me and, as I tried to move, I cried out and realized the whimpers had come from me. I didn't know how long I'd been asleep, but from what I could see through the small window, the sun was out. There wasn't a part of my body that didn't scream in pain.

But most of all, I could really use a drink.

I laughed at myself. After everything I'd been through, all I could think about was a drink.

Prying my tired eyes open once more, I tried to shift my body to the side, only to still.

Had I?

Yes, there were voices.

Someone was here.

I must have lost the plot because, even though it was faint, I was sure I heard Adrik's rough and gruff tone. I laughed at myself for that one.

A door slammed. Footsteps descended the porch above me. There *were* people here. I picked up the chains and rattled them. I banged them against the floor and opened my mouth to yell.

My voice failed me. A small sound fell out instead.

Were they leaving? They couldn't leave.

Please, please, help me. Please.

I cleared my throat and tried again. It stung, but it was

louder. Tears welled and dropped when no one came rushing back to the house.

The basement door opened, and I knew my chance to get free was shortening.

Opening my mouth, I ignored the pain and screamed with everything I had left in me.

Please, please, please.

They have him," Adrik shouted before he started for their front door.

"Fuck." Kylo went after him.

"Wade, I have to go."

Wade growled through the phone, "Don't you fuckin' dare—"

He would kill me for hanging up on him, but I had to follow the others after hearing that scream. The goose bumps still hadn't faded from when the sound pierced the air.

My heart was in my throat. Adrik didn't knock. No, he shouldered his way through the door, and it opened with a bang, hitting the wall behind it. He raced in, yelling, "West."

"You can't be in here," Grace screamed, coming at us from down a hallway with a rolling pin.

She was close to Adrik when he palmed her face and pushed her to the side. She stumbled, dropping the pin, and fell to the floor.

Kylo pulled a gun and aimed it at her. "Move, and I'll shoot."

"West?" I yelled.

"Where is basement door?" Adrik demanded from Grace.

She glared up at him, saying nothing, but he caught, like I did, the flick of her gaze to the side. Adrik started for the door. I followed. He swung the door wide and flew down the stairs.

I slipped on one when Adrik's roar echoed around the space. When I hit the last step, I stopped cold.

No. God, no. Oh my God, please no. Not West.

Adrik advanced on Harold, who backed up. I heard a snap as Adrik roared again. Harold's body dropped to the floor. Lifeless.

A sob broke free. I hadn't realized I'd walked over to West until I dropped to my knees beside my best friend, who flinched back with a whimper.

"West," I whispered.

"I'm not evil," he croaked.

"No, honey, you're not." Dryness caked around his lips, and there was vomit on the floor before him. He didn't even open his eyes. My tears fell while my heart shattered for him.

Adrik dropped to his knees on the other side of West. "Keys, find them," he demanded from me with a wave of his hand. I didn't move right away, so I saw the tears welling in his eyes.

"I'm clean. I am," West rasped.

I covered my mouth to stop the sob. Shaking my head over and over.

"Moya lyubov', ty prekrasnyy, dragotsennyy i n iodin nikto budut prikosnut'sya k tebe snova. Ya obeshchayu eto."

If my Russian was correct, he told West, "My love, you are precious, beautiful, and no one will touch you again. I promise this."

"Adrik?" West whispered.

"Da, Moya lyubov'. Rest, I am here."

West hummed, and his body lolled.

Adrik stood. After removing his jacket, he gently covered West's lower half. He couldn't touch West's back because… because…. I had never seen anything like it. His back had been sliced open, and a cross was burned into his skin. A fucking cross.

"Keys, Lucas. Now."

Wiping my eyes, I nodded. I got to my feet and went to the bench where a bloody knife, jugs with what smelled like vinegar and alcohol in them, and a cross on a long metal rod all sat.

"Keys, Lucas." Adrik demanded again.

I grabbed them and turned, seeing Adrik bent, whispering into West's ear while gently running his hand over his hair.

"Adrik," I called, and tossed the keys to him. He easily caught them. "I'll tell Kylo and search for some supplies to help."

Adrik nodded, and I could see how grateful he was I didn't try and get him away from West. "Da."

I made my way up the stairs. At the door to the basement, I stopped. Leaning my hands on each side of the doorway, I sucked in a breath and closed my eyes. How could someone do that? How could his own parents torture him like that? Bile rose. I swallowed it down.

"Lucas?" Kylo called.

Clenching my jaw, I looked up through watery eyes.

Kylo shook his head. "Lucas?"

"He needed to be cleansed" came a voice.

My anger erupted. I launched myself across the floor and wrapped my hands around her neck. "How could you? How fucking could you do that to him?" I shook her, heard her choking, but I didn't care. She deserved it. She deserved to die.

Hands gripped my shoulders. "Lucas, stop. She'll pay. She'll fuckin' pay, but tell me what she did. Tell me where West is."

I dropped back to my butt and scooted away from the monster. I swiped at my face. "They tortured him, Kylo. His back...." I shook my head, a sob catching in my throat. "They sliced him, burned him, branded him with a cross."

"Motherfuckin' cunt!" Kylo screamed. He aimed and fired. Blood pooled over her shoulder, the monster cried and cried, but I didn't care.

I stood and watched as Kylo pocketed his gun, picked up a side table, and smashed it onto the floor. It shattered. He took one of the broken leg pieces over to her and stabbed her in the thigh. She bellowed, but it tapered off into praying, then asking where her husband was.

Kylo turned to me. "She won't go anywhere."

"I need supplies. I'm going into the bathroom—" The front

door burst open, Wade filling it. Others were behind him. He started for me, but I took a step back. My bottom lip trembled. "No, don't. I... I have to hold on. I have to be strong for West."

"Babe," Wade said gently.

"No!" I shook my head over and over. "I need supplies. We have to get him out of here."

"What the fuck happened?" Country, the president of the Diamond MC, demanded.

"Adrik?" another man asked.

Closing my eyes, I took a deep breath and opened them again. "Adrik's in the basement with West. We can't call the police because he killed the father and that... that is the mother." I bit my trembling lip and took another breath. "She deserves pain. So much of it."

"Fuck," Saint uttered, going close to Kylo.

"I need supplies," I told them and walked away. I knew Wade would follow, but I needed him at a distance because I would crack. I would fall and let the sorrow fill me.

Still, I heard Kylo tell them what those bastards did to West, then something else got smashed into the ground.

I found a bathroom and opened the cupboards under the sink. My hands trembled as I searched for supplies. Inside, I found ibuprofen, antiseptic ointment, bandages, and gauze pads. It would have to do until I could get some more. Turning, I jumped when I spotted Wade standing in the doorway. How could he be so silent for such a big guy?

"Babe, are you okay?"

"It doesn't matter about me. Only West does right now." A

sob caught in my throat. He took a step until I shook my head. "Hold me *later*, please." I bit down on my bottom lip.

Wade nodded. "I will."

"How did you get here so fast?" I asked to keep my mind on other things.

"Adrik's guy woke. Told us an older lady had come up to him asking for directions when he stepped out of his car for a smoke. Didn't think to expect anything suspicious about an innocent woman looking for the right building. But also, Tech hacked into West's parents' phone records, finally. There was one text we didn't like so we were on our way to check these fuckers out."

Nodding, I sucked in another breath and straightened my shoulders. "All right." Wade moved out of the way, and I strode by, heading right for the basement.

On the stairs, I heard West cry out and then Adrik, "*Moya lyubov'*, I have you. It's okay."

I quickly walked down to see Kylo, Saint, Country, a man I didn't know but presumed was Dimitri, and State. Saint's hands were on Kylo's shoulders.

"Adrik?" West whispered in the quiet room as he leaned his side into the man who held him.

"Da, Moya lyubov'."

"Are my sins gone?"

Kylo dropped his head and gripped his hair. Country turned away, closing his eyes. It was State who swore, spitting, "Fuckin' hell."

"*Moya lyubov'*, you never had sins. You are perfect the way you are."

I ground my teeth together and kept breathing deeply in and out of my nose as I placed the supplies on the floor beside us.

"She said I was evil. I'm not evil."

"Nyet, you are not."

State shook his head and made his way out of the room. We all heard the monster upstairs scream out in pain.

I moved the water bottle aside; someone must have gotten him a drink. "West, it's Lucas. I'm going to put some cream on your back and wrap it up. I'll take a better look when we get you home."

He hummed under his breath. First, I checked his vitals. He had a steady heartbeat, but I could see he was dehydrated. Gently, I opened his mouth and paused. I let go of his jaw and asked, "West, did they pour something in your mouth?" It was red, so fucking red in there.

"Vinegar."

Adrik tensed, and our gazes met.

"Purge the sins away," West whispered.

Tears filled my eyes, but I blinked them away. Someone groaned. I glanced to see Kylo turned into Saint, with his head buried into Saint's chest. His body shook, crying silently. Saint's own eyes were wet. As was everyone's.

I brushed West's cheek with the back of my fingers. "My amazing friend, there were no sins to purge. There was nothing wrong with you. *They* were wrong." I picked up the pills and dropped three out. "Help him sit a little to take these," I said. Adrik did. "West, these are pain pills. You'll need to swallow them, sorry. I know it'll hurt, but they'll help a little."

He nodded and winced. Blinking again and again, he shook his head. "Tired."

"I know. You can keep your eyes closed, but you have to take these. Open your mouth for me." He did. I placed the pills in and helped him drink. He cringed when they slid down. I glanced to Country. "When I have him bandaged, we'll need to move him right away. Get him home, and I'll go to the hospital for things."

Country nodded. "We're set to go when you are. There'll be no witnesses. The other brothers will stay. They know what to do."

I went to work, and even though I hated myself for hurting him more, it had to get done. I had to keep going through his whimpers, his cries, and his begging for me to stop. By the end of it, he passed out.

"West," Adrik called, panicked.

I rested my hand on his arm. "It's okay. He's just unconscious. His mind is protecting itself."

His jaw clenched, but he nodded.

Looking to Wade, I ordered, "Find something we can use as a stretcher." Wade walked from the basement without a question. "We have to be very careful when we move him."

"Da,"

"Adrik, what do you want me to do?" Dimitri asked.

"Go to my parents. Tell them I won't be home. Tell them what happened."

Dimitri's lips thinned. "Do they—"

"They know. Take the men outside with you."

Dimitri nodded and left.

"You can go too—" Country started to say to Adrik.

"Do not say another fucking word," Adrik snarled. "I do not leave West's side."

"Don't!" The word came from me. Country's eyes were already on me when I looked up. "Adrik needs to stay."

"I agree," Kylo stated.

Country tipped his chin up. "Okay then."

"I killed the father too quickly," Adrik muttered, more to himself maybe. "He should have suffered for what they have done."

"He's burning in hell for it right now," Saint said.

"Not enough," Adrik clipped.

"No, it's not," Kylo agreed. "At least we have the other… cunt to rain pain on."

Adrik's smile was sinister. "She will learn just what they have done to him by doing it to her."

"He'll need boxers or something wrapped around his waist," I said.

"He can have mine," Kylo replied, already undoing his jeans.

"Jesus," my brother clipped. He pulled Kylo to a corner and guarded him so no other saw.

By the time Wade came back down the stairs with State, we had helped West into the boxers. They had found an ironing board, and even though it was old, it was wide and perfect. I nodded. "Good. We'll lift him gently and lay him on his stomach. It's going to be hard going up the stairs, but we can do this. I need at least four surrounding him at all times."

I was surprised when West didn't wake, only whimpered when we managed to get him on the ironing board. State, Saint, Country, and Adrik slowly carried West out, with Kylo following.

I needed a moment.

"Lucas," Wade said, his hand slid to my shoulder from behind me.

"They tortured him. Poured vinegar down his throat. Who does that?"

"Vile creatures."

"He didn't deserve that. No one does," I whispered. A heavy weight settled against my heart for my friend.

He applied pressure. "No."

"His own parents."

"I know."

I swallowed thickly. Tears brimmed and fell once again. "He'll need us all." I sucked in a deep, shuddering breath and straightened.

"And he'll have us." His hand slid across my shoulders, and he pulled my back into his chest. "Love you, babe."

"Love you always, Wade." I dipped my head down to kiss his arm. "Let's get him home."

He kissed the back of my head. "Where he belongs."

"Yes." He did. He belonged with us. We were our own little family, and we'd cocoon him in so much love and support. West would get through this. He would, but the path to it was going to be rough.

CHAPTER ELEVEN
ADRIK

My chest felt like it was torn wide open so everyone could see the split, bleeding, damaged heart, which only still beat for the man lying on his stomach on the mattress. A part of me wanted to crawl into the bed with West, curl myself around him, and protect him from the rest of the world for life.

No, that was not true. It was not a part of me that wanted to do it. It was all of me.

I could not get his screams out of my head from when we had carried him into the house. They rang through my mind over and over, along with all his others from when we had found him. Lucas had given him a mild sedative as soon as we got into the room. I never left his side the whole time, and I would stay always, ignoring the acid burning in my gut.

My sweet West did not warrant the treatment he went through. Fury lit under my skin, burning me with the thought of how his parents had done this.

"The church," I stated softly.

"What?" Kylo asked, also in a hushed tone, from where he stood beside me. I could feel Lucas's eyes on me from my other side.

"I will have my men investigate the church where those people attended," I answered.

Kylo hummed. "Good fuckin' idea. We need to make sure those two weren't the only cunts like that. I'm sure the brothers will help with that."

I nodded once. "We will work together."

"I-I need a shower," Lucas whispered. It had been hard on him assisting West with the wounds, but I could see the strength he held within himself.

"I will stay with him," I told Lucas.

"I'll go talk to the brothers about the church."

"Have someone speak with Dimitri when he returns."

Kylo gently slapped my back. "I will." He exited the room, quietly closing the door behind him.

Lucas stayed a little longer, and I waited him out, knowing he had something to say. He sucked in a shuddering breath. "I'm glad you were here today, Adrik. If you hadn't been, we might not have got to him in time. We might have walked away." He sniffed. "It'll be a long healing process, not only physically, but mentally."

"I will help him."

"I know you will. But what I'm saying is that he might not want you around when he wakes and is fully with it. He won't want to be a burden. He won't want you to see him like this. You'll need to be persistent."

"Nothing will have me leave him. Not now." *Not ever.* West was mine. If I had not been stubborn in the first place, none of this would have happened. I would have had him with me, at my side, protecting him. "I fucked up."

"How?"

"I should have gone after him sooner."

Lucas shook his head. "No one would have seen this coming."

"I could have. If I had come to him sooner."

"Don't blame yourself. West won't want that."

It was too late. Even so, I would do everything in my power to make it up to him.

"Do you—" I shook my head. "Never mind."

"No, you can ask or tell me anything."

I glanced down at him. Both Kylo and Lucas were good friends for West. No, they were more than that; they were his family. With the amount of time I had been around them, I could see the love they had for one another. I was glad West had that.

But I wanted to give him more.

I wanted to give him what Lucas had with Wreck or Kylo with Saint.

And, of course, I wanted that to come from me and no other.

"West has spoken of me?"

"Yes."

"So you know I was a client?"

"Yes."

"Would he want me to be around?"

He paused and bit his bottom lip in thought. Lucas would know what West thought about me. He would also know if deep down West wanted me.

When he nodded, I let out a heavy relieved breath. The gaping hole in my chest filled a little. "Good." Because nothing West could say would have me leaving him again. In some eyes, it might seem too soon for something between us. Nevertheless, I knew we had something special we could build on.

"I'll be back soon," Lucas said.

"Take your time. You know I will be fine here, and I will call if he needs anything medical."

"I know." He smiled, but it did not reach his eyes. I understood. Trauma took a lot from a person. He patted my arm before he walked out of the room.

There was an armchair in the corner of the room near the door with a few clothes. I removed the clothes, picked up the chair, and placed it next to the bed. When I accidentally landed it down a little heavy, I cringed and looked at West. Mercifully, he did not wake. What helped would be the drugs Lucas had a man from the brotherhood retrieve from the hospital—a call he made on the drive back to the house. Lucas had also set up fluids to help counter the damage the vinegar had done.

I closed my eyes, once more wishing I had not let the rage take me over when I saw West chained to the floor. If the father was alive, I would enjoy delivering pain to him slowly, like I would the mother.

My eyes flashed open when West moaned. His brows

drew down in his sleep; his breathing grew ragged. I knew a nightmare had taken him. Resting my chest to the edge of the mattress, I placed a folded arm on the bed, leaning onto it. I used my free hand to softly run over his sweat-beaded forehead. "I am here, moya lyubov'. No one has you. Sleep peacefully. I will stay here at your side to watch over."

Eventually, the tension eased from him, but I did not stop running my fingers through his hair. I dropped my head to rest on my arm. Lucas had gently washed his face while West had been passed out. His lips were redder than usual, and Lucas had told me inside West's mouth was the same. Irritated from the vinegar.

When West shivered, I pulled the sheet up and over his bandaged back. The sight of him kneeling on the floor swept through my mind, and I thinned my lips to keep the growl at bay. His wrist was also bandaged; his knees were covered in gauze pads protecting the deep scrapes. Bruises showed on his ribs, and the tops of his feet were grazed.

All of it told us he had tried to fight.

He would have been scared out of his mind. Traumatized to see these actions coming from his parents.

No, my West had done nothing to warrant what happened.

I would do everything in my power to make sure he lived his life in happiness and love.

A soft knock sounded on the door. I straightened, placing my fingers on the end of his to make sure West knew subconsciously someone was there with him. "Da?"

It opened, and Dimitri entered, closing it quietly after

himself. His averted gaze told me something was wrong. "What?" I barked and quickly glanced down to West. He stirred a little. Glaring over at my friend, I rested a finger to my lips. Dimitri nodded and shifted closer.

"Your parents are here."

I clenched my jaw. "Why?" I demanded in a harsh but quiet tone.

"Once I told them, they wanted to be here for you and West." He winced.

I whispered in a hissed low voice, "I do not need them—"

"Adrik," Dimitri clipped quietly. He took a step closer. "You know how convincing your father is, but most of all, your mother. She cried, Adrik. Cried once I told her what happened to West."

Fuck.

I should have anticipated it. My mother had the biggest heart out of anyone in the family. It was how father had softened, somewhat, over the years.

Another soft knock sounded. I lifted my chin toward the door, and Dimitri stepped back to open it. Lucas walked in, his hands in front of him rubbing together in nervousness.

"So… um… you might want to get out there. The brothers haven't taken too kindly to having the *Russian mafia boss* in the house."

"Fuck me," I cursed and glanced down to West.

"I'll stay with West, of course," Lucas said.

"I am sorry for this," I told Lucas as I stood.

"You can't help who your parents are." He smiled. "Wait until you meet mine. They're a bit overbearing." He winced.

"But probably nothing like what a mob boss is… or what West's were like… and I'll shut up now." West and Lucas were similar in some ways with talking when nervous. I could tell why Wreck was taken with him.

"I will not take long."

"Okay."

With Dimitri at my back, I walked through the house until I rounded the corner to the living room. There I stopped and took in the situation. My parents sat on the couch. Papa had his arm around Mama's shoulders as they leaned back into the seat. Papa was smirking at the men who stood around the room with their arms crossed, watching them.

Kylo was the only person who didn't seem concerned that my parents were here. He walked into the room with a tray of drinks and set them on the coffee table. He was handing one to my father when he noticed me.

"Here he is." He offered a tired smile.

"Adrik," Mama called. She stood and strode to me. I brought her into my arms for an embrace. "I'm so sorry for West."

I ran a hand up and down her back. "I know, Mama."

Papa stood, and everyone tensed. Their reaction did not surprise me. My father was well known. The stories of him killing men in seconds had spread over the world.

"Adrik, is there anything we can do?" Papa asked.

In Russian, I explained, "*No, not at the moment. He is resting, and I will stay here with him. I appreciate your concern, but there is nothing you can do.*" Mama pulled back to listen to us. I curled an arm around her shoulders.

"Those who did this to him, they have been dealt with?" Papa asked.

"I killed the man, but the other is still breathing. For now."

"Let me know if you need assistance. I would like to get my hands on a parent who would do this to their own child."

"I would also like to spend some time with her," Mama spat.

"She will pay," I reassured them. *"The men around you are also very protective and will seek vengeance on West's behalf. After I am done with her."*

Papa glanced around the room. *"They are a club?"*

I nodded. *"A brotherhood."*

Papa grunted. *"They fear me."*

I shook my head. Before I could say anything, Dimitri did with *"No, they are keeping an eye on their prey."*

Papa grinned. *"I might like them."*

A brief smile touched my lips. *"They are good men."*

"Right, this conversation none of us can understand has gone on long enough," Country, the club's president, stated, dropping his arms and fisting his hands at his sides. "Speak English or leave."

"We mean no harm. It is just easier for us to speak Russian in stressful times," Mama explained. Country nodded. She looked up at me. "We will leave. Please let us know if there is anything we can do."

"I will, Mama." I kissed her forehead before she moved to the side, and Papa stepped up for an embrace. "I will call."

"Da." Papa nodded. "For anything. We look forward to meeting West."

"But only when he's ready," Mama stated quickly. She

pointed to where a bag lay on the floor. "I took the liberty to pack you a few things."

"Blagodaryu vas, Mama."

She smiled warmly. "You're welcome."

"We will go now," Papa said, his arm outstretched to Mama, who walked over to him after another quick hug for me.

"Take Dimitri with you."

"No, Adrik. I will stay here also," Dimitri chimed in with a hard look my way.

"You do not need to stay."

"I am not stupid. You will send men away with your parents and have no one. I will stay."

I glared. Kylo spoke up. "He'll be safe here."

Wreck, who'd arrived at some point, snorted.

I rolled my eyes.

"He stays," Papa said, eyeing Wreck. "I will order the others to go with us." He knew and trusted that Dimitri and I were more than capable of taking on the room if needed. However, I knew nothing would happen, because I had Kylo and Lucas in my corner.

"Acceptable."

Once the door closed, I turned to the others in the room. "I know you do not know me. But I promise this, none of my father's work will disrupt your lives. He takes every precaution to not be seen when here or else he would not visit. He does not want to risk my mother or me."

"As long as it stays that way," State said.

"It will. I know this or I would not stay. I would not want anything from that side of the family to touch West."

"Speakin' of West," Death started. "What do you think is gonna happen between you two? As far as I knew, you were just a client who West wanted to get away from."

Dimitri stilled beside me. I glanced there and told him, "It is fine." His jaw clenched, but he nodded. I looked to Death again. "What West and I have is between us. I will not speak to anyone about it but him. However, I will let you know that I will be making West mine. If he will have me."

Silence answered me. I crossed my arms over my chest and waited them out.

"If he doesn't want anythin' to do with you, you gonna leave him alone?" Wreck asked. I curled my lip at him. I was not sure what it was, but there was something about Wreck I did not like.

"I would leave," I told him. "While West is here, though, you will have to put up with me staying."

"I could kick you out," he growled.

I dropped my arms and took a step forward. "I would like to see you try."

"Fuckin' hell, we get it. You two think you're the biggest and baddest out there," Kylo snapped. "But for fuck's sake, we're thinkin' of West." He pointed toward the hall. "And he will want Adrik to stay." Saint slipped up behind Kylo and placed his hands on his lover's sides. After he whispered something in Kylo's ear, Kylo sighed and nodded. "Look, this ain't my house. I can't say who stays or goes. But I have a feelin' that West will need Adrik."

Wreck's jaw clenched. "I don't like you," he said to me. "Stay until West says otherwise, and then I'll take great pleasure to kick you the fuck out."

I nodded. I was not in the mood to goad Wreck more, and I would leave willingly if West did not want me there. Turning, I stalked back toward West's room.

"What will you do while I am in here?" I asked Dimitri, sensing him behind me with his silent movements.

"I will guard the door."

"You do not have to stay. You know I can handle things."

"I know. But I will always have your back, Adrik."

Facing him, I clasped him on the shoulder. "And I appreciate it, friend." I ran a hand over my face. Weariness tugged at me.

"You know the ogre is only looking out for his partner. He protects, like you. He does not trust us because of the Mikhaillova name."

He spoke of Wreck. "I know this, and maybe I will come to like him, but right now is not the time." Until then, I would tolerate him. I would do anything for West and to be able to stay at his side.

CHAPTER TWELVE
WEST

Oxygen. I needed to breathe. I woke gasping for air but was unable to find it. I cried out as I tried to move, the pain radiating throughout my body.

"It's okay, you're all right. Just breathe with me. Come on, West. Look at me and breathe." A hand ran over my head. I flinched back, the voice not registering.

"No," I croaked and tried to move again. Pain slashed into me.

"It's Lucas, West. It's me, honey. I'm here. You're at home."

I stilled. "Lucas?" Opening my eyes, they focused on Lucas's face right in front of me.

"Hey," he whispered with a soft smile.

Tears pooled. "Lucas," I uttered, my breath catching in my throat. It stung as I swallowed over and over, but the emotions got the better of me, and I cried. I sobbed because I wasn't there.

They'd come for me.

I was home with my friends, my family.

I was free.

"Oh, honey, it's okay. You're all right. You're here," Lucas cooed. He touched his forehead against mine. "We have you."

They did.

I was home.

Where I was supposed to be.

After a shuddering breath, I opened my eyes to my best friend. "T-Thank you for coming for me."

"We always will. I knew something was wrong when you didn't come home or call. I got Wreck onto it right away, but we didn't have a clue where you were. I-I'm sorry it took so long."

"No. Don't apologize. N-No one… no one would have—" I closed my eyes, clearing my tender throat. "—thought my parents would do *that.*"

My body trembled over the reminder of it. The pain, the agony, the heartbreak. Their crazed eyes, the prayers. I never wanted to hear another prayer in my life. I thinned my lips to keep from crying.

I'm home. I'm home, I'm home.

"Adrik—"

Lucas had started until I opened my eyes wide. "He was there." It flashed back to me, hearing his voice. "I hadn't imagined him?"

Lucas shook his head. "No, he was there. Adrik was the one who heard you. He broke through the door to get to you and hasn't left your side since. Well, until his parents just arrived to check on him and you."

I bit my bottom lip to stop the tremble. I shook my head, tears welling once more.

"What? What is it? The pain meds should still be working. Do you need a drink, food?" Lucas straightened to check me over.

"He can't be here," I whispered.

Lucas paused. He went to his knees beside the bed and looked at me. "But why?" he asked.

It was difficult, but I lifted a hand, ignoring the stabbing pain in my back and wrist, and covered my eyes as the tears slid down. "He can't be here" was all I said again.

"West, honey, I don't understand. You left him because you didn't think he held anything for you. But anyone who was there could see he does. He cares for you a lot."

"He *can't*," I tried again.

"Why, West? Please make me understand."

I couldn't. Adrik wouldn't understand.

Closing my eyes, I shook my head.

"West, honey, I need to know before he comes back to your room because, believe me, he will come back. He doesn't like being far. He hasn't slept. The only reason he's not at your side now is because of his parents." I groaned when I shook my head again. "West, you know I love you. I do. And I know you have been through so much. You're in pain. There'll be a lot of healing ahead. But… and I'm going to be honest here, that man out there can help you. If you let him."

"No!" I choked.

"Hey, hey, it's okay." He ran a hand over my head gently. "It's okay. We'll sort it out. It's all right."

It wasn't.

Adrik was…. "He needs someone better." I pushed my hand harder onto my leaking eyes. "I'm not for him. I'm weak, dirty. I'm—" An anguished sob swept out of me.

"West," Lucas cried. "No, no, no. You are beautiful, amazing, and strong. Do not let them win."

They hadn't won. What they said didn't affect me. But their actions, what they did, had. I was scarred, damaged, no good. They had ruined me for him, for anyone.

The image of them burning the cross onto me pushed forward. It was so vivid I could almost smell my skin as it sizzled under the heat of the metal. I gagged, coughed, and fought for a breath.

"Breathe, West, breathe with me." Lucas's voice penetrated the memory.

A violent quiver raked over me as I sucked in the air and slumped from my elbows to lie flat on the bed.

"That's good. Breathe."

"Lucas," I heard.

I stilled, paling. My fingers gripped the sheets under me.

I watched Lucas's wide gaze turn to the doorway. "Yes?"

"Please get West a drink and some food," Adrik said.

Lucas flashed his gaze back to me and then to the door. "Um…." He straightened.

No. Don't leave me. Don't let him stay. I wanted to yell it, scream it, but I couldn't seem to bring myself to open my mouth.

"Okay?" He didn't look back to me before he rushed from the room, or he would have seen me pleading with my eyes.

I heard the door close and then soft footsteps. Once Adrik was beside the bed, he sat in the armchair. I took him in. He looked… well, exhausted. Stubble covered his cheeks, chin, and above his upper lip. His hair was wild, his clothes wrinkled. Nothing like I'd seen him before.

Wiping at my eyes, I blanked my expression even when inside me all I wanted was to cry more, to scream, plead for him to leave… and yet, I still wanted to slip into his arms and have him hold me for the rest of my life.

But I couldn't.

He sat on the edge of the seat and rested his forearms on the bed, bringing himself closer. "There are things I have to tell you."

My broken heart skipped a beat. "What?" I whispered, and all other thoughts evaporated because he sounded so serious.

His gaze roamed over my face. "My last name is not Hail. It is Mikhaillova." He paused as if he waited for a reaction, but it meant nothing to me. His gaze dropped to his clasped hands. "My family sees over many people in Russia. My father is in charge of the mafia there."

My eyes widened.

Adrik nodded when he took in my reaction. "Da, I was a part of the mafia, but I longed for something more. It is why I moved here. I cut ties with the family business, but not my family. I would do anything for them." His head cocked to the side, studying me. "Even though I am not part of what I left behind, there will always be a risk. Although we take many precautions that it will not touch my life now. It is the same when my parents visit."

He stopped, and I wasn't sure what he wanted me to say. Did he think it scared me knowing his family was in the mafia? It didn't. I was shocked but not scared. How could I be when my life already consisted of men in a motorcycle club who were ruthless in their own way. Besides, that was in Russia; it wasn't here. He'd cut ties with that side of things, that was what he said, and I believed him. I knew Adrik wouldn't have been accepted as a client by Polished if he was into shady things.

"Okay," I offered, not knowing what else to say.

A small smile touched his lips as he breathed out a light chuckle. It faded too soon, and he sobered with a frown. "There is something else."

"What?" I asked, my stomach knotting with tension.

He closed his eyes, jaw clenching. He pushed off the bed and leaned back in the seat, wiping his hands up and down his thighs. "I was blinded by rage. I could not stop myself even if I wanted to. Even if you had begged."

This didn't sound good. "Adrik, what?"

"I saw you on the floor and the man standing over you…. I killed your father."

Oh heavens.

Bile rose. I coughed.

"I know death is not the answer, but—"

"Stop," I ordered, sucking in a breath.

Adrik's lips thinned, but he kept his mouth closed. Worry drew his brows together.

"I'm not upset you did that," I told him honestly. I took a breath to steady my racing heart. There was no way I could be upset over it. The sight of me… of what they did, would be enough to anger anyone who knew me. Did it sadden me *he* was dead? No. Not in the slightest, and if that made me a bad person, then I would take it on, but I would never in a million years care about them.

I licked my dry lips. "What about *her*?"

"Are you sure you want to know?"

"Yes," I hissed. "I want to know what state she's in." I hoped she was in pain like I was.

"Lucas choked her. Kylo shot her and stabbed her leg. She has been beaten." He watched me, waiting. When I didn't react, he nodded and went on. "What was done to you, I will do to her before her life ends."

Again, he watched me, waiting.

I blinked slowly, suddenly tired. "Are you sure you want to do that? I mean, the club would take care of her for me."

"Nyet. It will be me." He glanced away and then back. "Do you wish to save her?"

"No," I blurted. I closed my eyes and then opened them with more tears welling. In a hushed tone, I asked, "Does… does it make me a bad person? Does it make me evil for wanting someone to die?" I bit my trembling bottom lip. Dread had my head spinning.

He leaned forward, taking my hand in both of his. "Nyet, moya lyubov'. Never. Not after what you have been through."

Still, guilt had me closing my eyes and shaking my head. *I shouldn't want someone to die.* But I did, and I couldn't find it in me to feel any remorse knowing my mother would die.

No, that wasn't right. She stopped being my mother when

she took the blade to my skin. Instead, they became… became—

"They were vile monsters, moya lyubov," Adrik said, as if reading my mind.

Opening my eyes, I uttered, "They were. But does it make me one when I want *her* dead?"

"Nyet, West. You had done nothing to them. You had been their son. They were supposed to care for you. They did not. They tortured you. They said it was for God, but it was lies. I will not let *her* get away with treating you as they did."

I raked my top teeth over my bottom lip as my heart thundered in my ears, and thoughts ran through my mind. "Can you do me a favor?"

"Anything." He sounded so adamant it made my chest hurt from the way my heart fluttered to life.

"Don't tell me what happens.… I don't want to know anything more about her. I-I'm just glad to know she suffered already."

He lifted my hand and kissed the back of it, causing my heart to react again. Only that time, my stomach fluttered right along with it.

"I will do this." He ran his thumb over my skin on my hand. I couldn't help but watch the movement.

Why was he there? Why would he do this for me? Why would he kill for me?

Those were questions I wasn't ready to hear the answers for.

Instead, I asked, "How did you find out my name?"

He winced. "I have something else to confess."

Oh.

"What?" I asked softly.

He took a breath and released my hand. I missed the contact instantly, which wasn't good, as in the end, I'd have to push him away.

He leaned back once more and glanced to the door. "I had a man watching you."

My stomach dropped. "Why?"

He met my gaze. "That is for another time. But know it was in your best interest."

"Adrik, you can tell me now."

"Nyet, your food and drink will be here soon, and you are not ready."

Not ready?

I didn't understand.

"I will be staying in this house," he announced instead, which threw me from any other thoughts.

"Why?"

He smirked. "Because."

"Because? That's all you're going to say?"

"For now." He stood, bending, and I closed my eyes when I felt his lips press into my temple. "Rest, moya lyubov'."

"What does *that* mean?"

He pulled back a little. "Moya lyubov'?"

"Yes."

His hand slid over my hair. "One day, I will tell you. But you need rest to heal. If you need me, I will not be far." He straightened and started for the door.

"Adrik?" I called.

"Da?"

"Thank you… for saving me."

"I will always save you, West. From anything."

I felt he meant more by that, but I couldn't work out what. He opened the door, and I heard Lucas's squeak. "Hello… um, you're leaving?"

"Is there a room I can take as my own?"

"Yes, of course. One right next door to here."

"Thank you."

"You're welcome." Lucas moved into the room, and I listened to the door close once more as Lucas stopped at my side. He set a tray on the bedside table. "I brought soup and a straw, so you won't have to move much to drink it." He sat on the chair. "How did that go?"

"Confusingly."

Lucas smiled. He picked up a bowl and stuck a straw in it, bringing it to my lips. "It's not too hot."

I took a gulp before I pulled back. "I… I think he likes me," I confessed. Everything he'd done and was still doing pointed in that direction.

Lucas threw his head back and laughed. Once he stopped, he ignored my glare and said, "Whatever gave that away?"

"Lucas," I whispered urgently. "I can't have him liking me."

Lucas's smile saddened. "From what I can tell, it's too late for that."

It wasn't too late. I had to make sure of it. Adrik needed someone who wasn't damaged, and I would push him to find that person, because it wasn't me.

CHAPTER THIRTEEN
ADRIK

He needs someone better. I'm not for him. I'm weak, dirty.

Those words seared my mind as I lay in bed. Neither West or Lucas knew I had been standing in the doorway and that I'd heard. My chest ached at those words. I wanted to drag West into my arms and tell him he was all I needed. Despite knowing he wasn't ready to hear it.

Instead, I would stay and worm my way into West's life in other ways. I would have him see me as the man who would be there for him, and eventually, he would not be able to deny what we could build on between us.

Rolling, I stared at the wall that separated us. The house was quiet since most of the men had left. I'd even sent Dimitri home to sleep, after I promised I wouldn't leave the house. I thought sleep would pull me under quickly, but it had not. My worry for the man in the next bedroom was too pronounced.

How could West think I needed someone better when all I

saw was him? Eventually, he would understand he was not weak or dirty. He was perfect, even with his new scars.

I had an urge to go to him, but he needed space.

Tomorrow, I would finish this for him. I would end the woman's life and take pleasure in delivering her pain as she had. I had no doubt she'd been the one who had inflicted the agony on West. He was in and out of sleep on the drive to the house, and his mumbled words had begged his mother to stop.

Sitting up, I rubbed at my chest as the fury lit inside me. Waiting was not a strength I had. I had a need to wrap my hands around her neck and wait as the life bled out of her.

There were only a few lives I had taken, and all meant something. All had been to save another.

With a sigh, I flicked back the blankets and put my feet to the floor. I wished I could sleep. However, my mind refused to shut down enough for me to do so. Instead, I stood and pulled on my pants. I zipped the fly but did not bother with the button. After walking to the door, I opened it and stepped out, closing it behind me. I could not lie in that bed any longer. I had to do something, and I was sure Lucas had said there was a gym in his large house somewhere.

I took a couple of steps, then paused. A sound from inside West's room had me pressing my ear against the door. He whimpered.

Would he want me to check on him?

Would he want me to ease him from his nightmare?

A shuffle from down the hall had me looking that way. Lucas stood with Wreck at his back.

"I thought he would have nightmares."

"Da, it sounds as if it has started."

Lucas nodded, frowning, while Wreck just glared. "Are you going in?"

Wreck gazed down at his partner but said nothing.

A scream ripped through the house.

"Da," I called and opened the door before me. I walked to the bed and sat on the edge at West's hip, resting my hand on his shoulder. "Shhh, moya lyubov'. You are not there. You are home. With your friend Lucas. Shh. Nothing will hurt you here." I hummed a tune my mama used to sing when I was a little boy while I ran my hand over the top of his shoulders, neck, and hair. He settled, his breathing evening out. "Good, moya lyubov'. That is it, breathe easy. You are not there, but here with me." I continued humming.

After a while, West whispered, "What's that song?"

I stilled for a second but then resumed tracing my fingers over him. "It is a song my mama used to sing to me when I was little and had nightmares."

"It sounds pretty."

"It is, and she has a beautiful voice."

"I wish I had someone like that for a mother."

I paused a moment. "Sorry, moya lyubov'. I wish you did also."

"Tell me more about your childhood."

"I am not sure it is a good idea."

"Please. I know mine was shit. They were strict, and as punishment, I had to read from the bible in the basement without supper. It was why, when I got the scholarship, I got out of there. I got away from them. I knew my upbringing was a lot different to others, but I still like to hear about normal families."

I snorted. "I would not call my family normal."

"How?" he asked, and the more I was around him, the more I found it hard to say no.

"I said my family is mafia. I was brought up knowing this. When kids my age had sleepovers, I had defense lessons. Older, when kids were going out drinking, I was learning to kill a man with my bare hands. But I never went without. I always knew my parents would do anything for me, and they loved me."

"Are you an only child?"

"Nyet. I have two older brothers, which was why it was easier for my father to let go. If I had been only child, I would have obligation to run business." I knew I missed words to speak better English, but I was tired. "They want it more. I never did."

"I'm glad you got to do what you want, Adrik."

"Thank you, moya lyubov'."

"Are you going to tell me what that means?"

"Nyet," I teased with a small chuckle. "Are you ready to sleep again?"

He tensed.

"West?"

Shifting, I glanced down at his face. He had his eyes screwed shut, but I still caught the tears that escaped. Fear had taken hold. He worried about sleeping and the nightmares that came with it.

"My brothers are dickheads," I announced. Before I pulled back and resumed my movements with my hand, I caught him relaxing somewhat.

He cleared his throat. "How?"

"Being the youngest, they always picked on me. But eventually, they stopped when I beat both of them in a fight. They still have moments, of course."

His laugh was light, but it cut off with a wince. "Of course," he said softly.

"My parents are in town at the moment."

"Lucas said."

"I am unsure how long they will stay."

"It must be good to have them here." He blinked tiredly.

"Da, it is."

"Do you need to go and spend time with them?"

"Nyet, they know I will be here."

"You don't have to—"

"Hush, moya lyubov'. Maybe when you are feeling better, you could meet them."

He swallowed thickly. "Maybe."

He needs someone better. I'm not for him. I'm weak, dirty.

His words rushed through my mind again. He would not want to meet them until he realized he was my someone. Until he saw he was not weak or dirty.

"Um… what about work?"

"I have many men who take care of things." *I am where I need to be,* I wanted to add but did not. He was not ready for my honesty. "I started reading those books."

"Yeah? What do you think?" He yawned, and I knew I would have to leave soon, even when I did not want to.

"You were right. They do get better with each one."

He smiled. I loved seeing it, loved that I put it there.

"Told you," he mumbled.

"Da, you did." I spoke about the characters, the storyline, and where I thought it would go. I talked and talked until I noticed his breathing had evened out. "Sweet dreams now, moya lyubov'," I whispered, and bent close to press my lips gently to his temple.

Only when I stood, West jerked and gasped, "Adrik."

I sat back down. "Da?"

"Nothing, sorry."

"I thought you had fallen asleep?" I questioned.

"I had... but I felt the bed move. Sorry, it's nothing. Goodnight."

"West, may I rest on the chair beside your bed?"

"No! Please don't feel you have to—"

"Hush." I pressed a finger to his lips.

They moved under my finger when he said, "I don't want to be a burden. You've already done enough."

"Moya lyubov'. You will never be a burden. Trust me. I would like to stay."

A blush hit his cheeks. He was always cute. "Then, in that case, take the other side of the bed. I... um, don't move much."

My gut twisted in the best way. "Thank you. I would like that." It could help me sleep also, being close to him. I stood again and moved around the bed. West turned his head my way. With a wave of my hand, I gestured to my pants. "Do you mind?"

The blush was back.

"No," he blurted quickly. He closed his eyes, and I removed my pants, slipping under the sheet. He opened his eyes as I lay down on my side, facing him.

"Do you need anything? I should have asked already."

"No." He smiled. "Lucas has me on the good stuff."

Reaching out, I pushed his hair from his eyes. "Goodnight, West."

"Night, Adrik." He closed his eyes and relaxed into the bed. I did the same, and as I suspected, it did not take me long to find slumber being beside moya lyubov'.

"Hold her," I ordered Wreck, of all people, and as he did, I gripped her jaw, prying it open. "You will feel everything you inflicted upon your son." I smiled down at her tear-streaked face as she tried to wiggle free, whimpering. Wreck's hold on her was steady, though. I rested the tip of the vinegar-filled jug to her lips. "You deserve everything you get."

She choked and coughed through the amount I forced into her. Once done, I stepped back, and Wreck released his hold. She slapped her hands to the floor, heaving as she vomited it up. I knew her throat would be burning; it brought a small smile to my lips.

She needed to suffer.

"Can you do the rest?" Wreck asked from over the other side of her.

Lifting my hard gaze, I told him, "Of course I can."

"Even when she's a woman?"

"Gender does not interfere when it comes to revenge. Not when she tortured her own son for being gay."

The bitch spat to the side. "It wasn't only that," she rasped.

"What?" I demanded.

Wreck kicked her in the back when she didn't answer, causing her to cry out. "Answer him."

"He whored himself out," she said.

Wreck chuckled. "You stupid bitch. He got paid to go on dates, and that was all he ever did. He never sold his body."

I had guessed as much, but it was good to know for certain nothing had happened with West's other clients. However, I still disliked the thought of West around other men. It would be something I had to work on *if* he continued working.

"It doesn't matter. He sinned."

I ground my teeth together and sneered down at the vile creature. Turning, I picked up the long, sharp knife and faced her. "Tie her hands down."

Wreck grabbed the chain connected to the wall and dragged it over to her. She backed away from him.

"No, stop, please. Don't do this."

I'd known it would not take long for the begging to start.

"Did your son plead for you to stop?" I asked, tapping the blade onto my other hand.

She sobbed and nodded.

Wreck used the chains around her wrist to pull her

forward where she lay on her stomach. "Then," I started, "do you think I will listen when you did not with West?"

"Please, please," she cried over and over.

"Hold her legs down."

Wreck nodded and moved around as I planted a foot on each side of her hips. She started praying. I laughed. "May the Lord condemn your soul to hell for what you have done." Leaning over, I sliced up through her top, and I did not stop there. The blade easily cut through the skin of her back, which welled with blood. She screamed and thrashed until I pressed my hand down onto the back of her neck. She still cried, but her movement stilled except for her hands as she hit them into the concrete floor while I sliced more and more of her skin.

Satisfaction swelled inside me, knowing she suffered the same way West had.

I had left him in the early hours to fulfill the revenge that burned inside me. I would go back to him knowing the last of the people who harmed him was dead.

I would make sure no other put a hand on him.

He would live the rest of his life happy and free from any harm.

And possibly, if I had anything to do with it, by my side.

Standing, I flung the knife to the floor. I stepped over her and made my way to the burning pit the Diamond MC men brought in for this situation. I picked up the searing metal rod and walked back over to the whimpering woman on the floor.

Ignoring her wide eyes, her imploring, I pressed the cross into her back. I winced as her skin sizzled and burned. It was not because of what I did. No, instead, it was the thought of West's agony when they had done this to him.

I clenched my jaw and held it longer, forcing it deeper into her flesh.

She had done this. She had hurt West. For that, she would get more than what she gave him.

Straightening, I pulled the cross from her back. Her skin stuck to it.

"Are you done?" Wreck asked.

I shifted my gaze to his. "She will feel more?"

He nodded. "She will. They won't hold back."

"I am done," I told him and made my way to the door. It had been a deal I struck with the Diamond MC. I got to deliver everything back to her exactly as she'd done to West, and in return, once I was done, they got to have their own fill of revenge.

Opening the door, Kylo, Saint, Country, and Death stepped through. They greeted me with a lift of their chin, but it was Kylo who patted me on the shoulder as he passed.

I heard a clap as I stepped through the doorway, and then someone said, "Wake her up and let's get this started."

CHAPTER FOURTEEN
ADRIK

imitri drove me back to my home. I did not want to show at West's covered in his mother's blood.

"How are the businesses?" I asked, scrolling through emails since I had already washed my hands at what Wreck had called the compound.

"Antony has everything under control."

I nodded. "Thank you for finding him." I knew I had said it before, when Antony had come on as a manager for the casinos, but he had been worth every penny since he started two months ago.

"You know I did it so you would have a break."

"Da, at least I am now."

Dimitri snorted. "Time off is not sitting there checking your emails. Besides, you have only been gone a few days. I will see if it lasts."

I grunted. Everything in me itched to get back to work. I knew I wouldn't until West was on his feet.

"Is there anything I need to know about?" I asked.

"Nothing. Honestly, you just worry about… your love."

Slowly, I glanced at him to see his smirk. "Are you really taunting me while I have blood on my clothes?"

"I have faith you will not harm me."

"If you say anything more about West, do not trust the faith you have."

"Got it," he replied with a smile. I went back to my emails. "Seriously though, it is good to see, Adrik."

"See what?"

"You finding someone."

"It is not set in stone," I informed him. Worry still twisted inside me that West would not want me to be a part of his life.

"Although—"

"Dimitri, you know I care for you like a brother. Better than my brothers. But I would prefer not to speak of this for now." I could not allow myself to think of a future for West and me as yet. I needed him healed. Needed him to understand I would not run, no matter what he thought of himself. Most of all, everything that had happened to him was still too fresh for me, and anger brimmed close under my skin to a point I would rip another's throat out if they said one wrong word about him.

"I understand," Dimitri said as he pulled into the underground parking area.

"Thank you," I told him when he parked. I exited and walked toward the elevators; the guards visibly stilled when they saw the blood on me. Ignoring them, I swiped the card and waited for the doors to open as Dimitri stopped at my side.

"Will we be here long?"

"Nyet. I want a shower and to pack more items."

"I shall take the time to shower also. I will meet you on your floor," he explained as we entered the elevator.

"Let my parents know I am here for a moment."

"I will. They will want to see you."

I nodded. "Give me ten minutes."

"Done."

Dimitri got out on his floor, and I went all the way up to mine for a much-needed shower. After, I stood out on my balcony in the midmorning sun, sipping a bourbon straight.

"*Vodka is always better, son. Do not let your mother catch you drinking that,*" Papa said in Russian as he walked out to stand beside me.

"*Where is Mama?*"

"*In our rooms. I wanted a chance to speak with you.*"

I rested my hip against the balcony and faced him. "*What about?*"

He gazed out over the scenery in thought. I took the time to finish my drink and set the glass on the ground before straightening and waiting some more.

"*Was I a bad father?*"

The shock from the question had my head jerking back. "What? Nyet."

He hummed under his breath.

"*I know our lives weren't... normal, but had I acted too cold, where you thought you couldn't come to me about things?*"

"You were strict but never cold. What has brought this on?"

He looked at me. *"Why had you never come to me, to your mother and I, and told us you preferred men? Did you feel you had to run to another place in the world to live how you wanted? Why did you feel you had to hide?"*

Fuck.

"It was never anything you or Mama did. It was what surrounded us. I felt it easier to keep it to myself, and in a way, I did not want to burden either of you. I did not feel I could be myself in Russia. I have even found it hard here also. Until I met West."

"I would have killed anyone who would have said anything back home."

I sighed and scrubbed a hand over my face. *"Even your other sons? Both have made comments about gay men. They have shown their distaste, and I never wanted you or Mama to be put in a position to take sides. I would also like to keep this from them as long as I can."*

"They are idiots sometimes, but they would have supported you in the end. Still, I will not say anything. I never would."

"Thank you." I glanced over his shoulder. *"Our lives were always different, and I knew coming out would have tarnished the family business."* I met his gaze. *"You know this."*

He spat to the side and snarled, *"They are all imbeciles to think I would not have fought them all to make sure you had a happy and safe life."*

"I would never want war between you and your people. It was better if I took myself out of the equation. It was hard to leave, but it was the better choice."

"It has been hard to have you away. We miss you."

"*As I do you and Mama.*"

"*In spite of you keeping this from us, in a way, I understand your reasoning. I only wanted to make it clear what I said the other day. You have our love, no matter who you love. We will always be here for you.*"

My heart clenched.

"*Thank you, Papa. I love you both also and always.*"

He grunted and slapped me on the shoulder. "*I am also proud of you, what you have built here for yourself. You have done well, Adrik.*"

"*I am happy.*"

He scoffed. "*I have seen a small glimpse of your happiness where your West is concerned. But before that, nothing. Do not let work run your life. You run it and make sure you grab that happiness you have found to keep it.*"

"*If he will have me.*"

"*He would be foolish not to have my son.*"

"*Only a father would say that.*"

"*A father who is always right.*"

I chuckled.

"*If you wish, I could have a talk to this West and see where he stands for you.*"

Christ no. "*I appreciate the thought, but that will never happen.*" Thinking of West had me wanting to leave, to see him, hold him.

"*Your mother and I would like to meet him before we go back.*"

"*He is healing.*"

"*In a week then.*"

"*I will see how he is then.*"

He paused for a moment. *"Your mother will take care with him when we do meet him."*

"I know."

"I will also... behave."

I snorted. *"We will see when it happens."*

He gave me another slap to the shoulder. *"Go. I can see you want to get back to him. See your mother on the way out, though."*

A small smile tugged at my lips. *"I will. Lock up when you leave."*

"Of course. Talk soon."

Nodding, I picked up my glass and made my way inside, eager to leave. Yet, I was going with a new lightness inside me. I had not realized I needed that conversation, but I appreciated my parents more than I ever had.

Using the code Lucas had given me, I unlocked the door to the house and stepped through with my bag. It was quiet since it was only Lucas and West here. The others were obviously still at the compound.

"Are you going to let me through?" Dimitri asked.

"You do know I do not need you here."

"I know, but I am your head of security and friend. I am not leaving you to deal with a bunch of bikers on your own."

"I am capable."

"That I also know. Maybe I will get bored without you. Maybe I will miss you."

"Father had you go with me."

"I shall be in the living room working." He stalked off with his computer case over his shoulder.

I had been correct about my assumption. Papa was the only other person Dimitri would listen to. I knew Dimitri trusted the other men from the Diamond MC, but it was Papa who was wary, and to ease his concerns, I would have Dimitri at my back during the daylight hours.

There would be no reason to send Dimitri on his way. I did not care if he stayed around the house. It also meant that while I spent time with West, he would be close if any business problems arose.

Walking through the house, I rounded the corner to the hallway where our bedrooms lay and saw Lucas pacing outside West's room. I dropped my bag to the floor and stalked toward him. When he saw me, he stopped and ran his hands together in front of him. His eyes were red.

"What is wrong?" I demanded and went to open the bedroom door. His hand on my arm stopped me.

"He's not in a good mood."

"What does this mean? Why does that stop me from going in? Why do you look worried?"

"He's in pain and not thinking. He's talking of going somewhere else to live because he doesn't want to be a burden. He's pissed about everything. I'm worried he'll do something stupid like try and move out."

"Then we will stop him."

"I've never seen him like this before. I mean, I can understand why he's in a foul mood, but... I don't know. I'm just worried."

"We will not let him wallow. He will need us even through his moods."

"He told me to get the fuck out, or else he was going to call someone to get him out of the house."

I ground my teeth together. I knew West would regret everything he had said to Lucas. I did not like seeing him upset his friend, his family. I had to do something, and if it meant West would be angry with me and only me, then so be it.

"Go and eat. I will see to him."

"But—"

"Lucas, do not worry."

He kicked at the carpet. "I just don't want you to see him in a mood and think he's not worth it in the end."

I rested a hand on his shoulder. "You are a good friend, but know this, nothing he says or does will have me feeling different about him. He is scared, in pain, and only has time to think. None of it will be good for him. With time, we will have our West back."

Lucas sucked in a breath and nodded. "Okay. All right. I'll go get something to eat."

"Da." I watched him leave the hallway and head for the kitchen before opening the door to West's room.

"Leave," West demanded.

"Nyet."

"I don't need you or Lucas hovering around me all the damn time."

"That is too bad."

He growled under his breath. "Just fucking leave. I don't

want you here. I never wanted you. It's why I left in the first place."

The words hurt a little, but I knew them not to be true. Not when Lucas had said otherwise.

"Is there anything you need?"

"No, get out!" he screamed and got to his elbows, but his face pinched from the pain, and he dropped back down. "I want to be alone. I don't want to see you again. Go back to your life, Adrik."

"I will be back in a moment," I told him.

He groaned, and as I walked from the room to grab my bag, he yelled, "Don't."

Picking up my bag, I made my way back into West's room and placed my bag beside me as I sat on the chair. West glared at me. "I want you to leave."

Ignoring him, I bent, unzipped my bag, and pulled out a book. "I am on the second-last book. I thought I might read it to you."

"I don't want you to," he snarled through clenched teeth.

I opened to the start, even though I was halfway through, and started reading.

"Why are you doing this? Why can't you get it through your thick Russian head that I don't want you here?"

I went on reading.

He groaned. "Jesus, you think you're that important? You're not. Go away. Go back to your family." He paused for a reaction, but when I didn't give him one and looked back to the book, he added, "This is my room. I want you gone. You have to listen to me. Fucking listen to me!"

Glancing back to the book, I opened my mouth to continue reading but stopped when West whispered, "Why are you doing this? Why won't you listen?"

"Because I care for you. As do Lucas and the others. No matter how much you hate yourself, we like you even more."

His breath hitched. "Please leave."

"Nyet, West," I said softly, and then went back to reading. He said no more and eventually drifted off to sleep. There was nothing he could say that would have me leave him, not when his mind would be playing tricks on him, telling him things, wrong things.

He needed me.

He needed us all, and we would be there for him. Through everything.

CHAPTER FIFTEEN
ADRIK

A week later, I stepped into the living room from being in West's room early morning. It had been the same the last few days—where I spent my days working on the businesses—but at night, I returned to West's room to read, talk, and sleep. Even when he never responded to me. After the first night, he had taken to ignoring me when he had asked me to leave, and I refused.

"Lucas, he would like to see you. He said it was something medical."

"On it." Lucas smiled, but it was not fully there. It hadn't been present since West had fallen into his anger. We tried to talk to him about seeing someone professional to speak with, but he refused each time. Unless he was asked a direct question or wanted something, he didn't seek conversation otherwise.

All of us were worried.

Had they gotten to him? Had they planted their seed into his mind, which had grown into something bigger?

He refused to get up, to move, only to lie there and allow himself to fall deeper into this state of despair. We could no longer see the person West had been. He did not argue. He did not invite people to see him. He did not want to see anyone. If it was not for Lucas, Kylo, Wreck, and me being persistent, West would have his way and be alone. We ignored his verbal abuse and spoke to him as if he had not said anything harsh at all.

The others were worried that it would be more harmful for West and his mental state if they kept coming back. It did not stop them from dropping into the house to check on him, though. West had so much support, so many cared for him. He was yet to see through his misery to notice it.

West had been through a lot. We could understand his anger, his pain, his fears.

All we had to do was wait it out to get our West back. And he would come back to us. Every now and then, he would say something hurtful and wince. Regret would shine in his eyes before he forced it down.

I did not understand the anger he showed Lucas and Kylo, though. They were his family. I was new in his life, so I expected him to try and push me away. Why was he with his family too?

"You okay?" Dimitri asked from where he sat on the couch. He had been here every day, only leaving at night when he knew Wreck was home. Somehow my friend had come to like the man I was still yet to not want to punch in the face.

"I will be. Anything I need to know?" I asked like I did every morning.

"Nyet. Go eat, or even better, have a shower. You stink. Then we will talk shop."

"Lies. I do not stink. What about my parents?"

"I know you feel guilty over not being with them, but you saw them yesterday. They are still the same, I am sure."

"They should go home."

"You know they won't until they meet West."

Crossing my arms over my chest, I glanced out the window behind the couch. "I am unsure when that will be or *if* it will happen."

"You are not giving up."

"Do not dare," I snarled.

Dimitri smiled. "There is the Adrik I know. Your man has been through a lot. I know you know this, but maybe a reminder will help you understand that he will get through this stage."

"I know," I said softly. Only, I hated that West hurt, not only physically but mentally. I hated seeing him in any pain, and I hated that it looked like I could not do anything about it.

I wished he would reach out to me, talk to me, let me know what he was thinking.

If he did, I could help.

Shaking my head, I made my way into the kitchen for coffee.

Kylo would be here soon to take over while Lucas was at college, so I made sure to get a fresh pot ready for him. I had been sitting with Dimitri going over a few things when a scream ripped through the house. I stood and bolted toward West's room. Lucas stood down the hall from it, at the bathroom door with his hands pressed against it. Towels and clothes were at his feet.

"What?" I demanded, stopping beside him. Dimitri stood at my back.

"He's locked the door. Won't let me in. He wanted a shower and… and since his back was healing okay, I thought it would do him good, but he won't let me in. I don't know what's happening."

"Move," I ordered.

When Lucas stayed where he was, Dimitri stepped up behind him and gently shifted him out of the way. Crying started from within the bathroom. I lifted a foot and kicked in the door.

"Get out, get out, get out," West chanted in a scream.

I stepped through the steam, already knowing what he had done. My heart splintered at seeing West naked and kneeling on the floor in the shower with the hot water running over him.

"Get out!"

Even though he was not looking at me, I shook my head. "Nyet, moya lyubov'." I pulled my T-shirt over my head and threw it to the floor.

"Get out," he cried. A whimper followed. Even under the waterproof gauze, his back's skin was raw from the heat of the hot water splashing down over him. *"Please,* please leave me. I-I'm dirty."

My chest cracked open as I shoved my jeans down my legs and opened the shower door. I stepped in, only wearing boxers.

A sob sounded behind me. Lucas.

"Moya lyubov', I will not leave you," I told him softly.

"You have to. I'm broken."

"Nyet." I leaned over him, sticking my arm in the scorching water, wincing. I quickly added cold to it, adjusting it to where it should be before I crouched at his side. "You may feel broken, moya lyubov', but you will heal."

He shook his head. I sat on the floor at his side, my legs around him.

"I'm no good. I-I don't want you to see me."

"Why?"

He choked on his cry, rocking back and forth on his knees. I rested a hand to his lower back, and he stilled.

"I'm n-no good. I'm tainted, tarnished, scarred. I-I wished they'd sent me to God."

Christ.

I cupped the opposite side of his neck and gently tugged him my way. He did not expect the move, so he fell my way. When his side pushed into my chest, I held him close. "Please, moya lyubov', do not say that. Do not wish your life away because of what *they* did to you. You are cared for. You have a family, friends, a life worth living. Let us in. Let us show you what you would miss. Let us help you through this."

He gripped my forearm, and I felt him shake his head. "I can't."

"Why?"

A whimper escaped him. He shook his head again, and I knew he cried even when I could not feel his tears.

"I-I don't deserve it."

"That is not true, moya lyubov'. I wish you could see you the way I do. No one has ever captured my attention in moments like you have. You are kind, funny, sweet. There is nothing but light within you, West. You deserve nothing but the best for the rest of your life, and I know that if you give us all a chance, we will make sure you have it." I ran my hand over his hair. "You will have scars, you will remember what they did, but you will get through it and know you *are* strong. You lived through hell and came out the other side. You will wear your scars with pride. They are a part of you, and there is *nothing* about you that is bad, tarnished, or tainted."

"Adrik," he whispered.

I kissed the top of his head. "I worry this is not the time and that it may be selfish of me, but I need you to know why I had a man watching you. You see, moya lyubov', I could not let you go. Even when you walked away, I could not stop thinking of you. I had to see how you were. Before you, it felt like I was a robot going through each day as they came. I did not see the world until you walked into my home. I regret I left it so long."

His hand tightened on my arm. "Don't blame yourself."

"I will try, as I hope you do the same for you."

He nodded against me and cleared his throat. "I-I want to talk to someone."

I closed my eyes, and my skin broke out in goose bumps. Hope blasted into me. "We will find the perfect person."

"Okay."

Everything would take time. I wanted to tell him more, but I had already said enough for now.

"Let me help you from the shower?"

"Can I... I need to wash."

"Drop to your ass. I will assist. As long as you are okay with this."

He lifted up. The pain etched onto his face hurt my heart. He nodded. "Please."

Slowly, we eased him to a sitting position, and I stood, picking up a washcloth. I held it behind me. "If you want to cover yourself," I offered. The washcloth was taken, and I grabbed the shampoo. Moving to his side, I adjusted the spray from his body. "Drop your head forward a little. I wash it so none of it reaches your back and makes it sting." Though, it looked raw still from the water before.

"Thank you," West whispered, dropping his chin down to his chest.

"Anything, moya lyubov'."

"What does it mean?"

"Anything but that," I teased, and was rewarded with a snort. I squirted some shampoo onto my hand and placed the bottle onto the floor. I lathered it up between my hands and knelt beside him. Gently, I rubbed it through his hair, and

West let out a contented sigh. Finally, he relaxed his tense form.

Something I said had gotten through. Happiness did not describe my feelings. He was letting me help. Letting me be here for him.

After rinsing the conditioner from his hair, I could not resist leaning forward and pressing my lips to the back of his neck.

"What was that for?" he asked softly.

"Because I had to."

"You had to?"

"Da."

He shook his head. "How can you look at me? Look at my back? Be close to it?"

I threaded my fingers through the back of his hair and gently tugged it to the side to have his eyes. I knew mine were hard from not liking his words. "I can look, I can see, because I do not lie when I say your wounds show me how strong you are. Your wounds are a part of you, and I like you, West."

"You shouldn't."

"You may think that, but it does not change how I feel." Leaning in, I kept his gaze and touched my lips to his jaw. His breath shook as he released it. "It is time to get out now."

"Okay," he uttered.

Slowly, I helped West stand. He kept the cloth in front of him, but it dropped when he stood.

A deep blush hit his cheeks when his hands landed on my chest, and he gazed up at me.

I smirked. "I won't look… much."

"Adrik," he clipped.

A laugh escaped me. "If you lean against the shower wall with your hands, I will retrieve the towel and boxers." He did, and I quickly slipped out of the shower and used a spare towel to dry off swiftly. I took the other back into the shower. I swallowed thickly as I allowed my gaze to run below his back. His ass was round and perfect.

"Do you wax?" I asked, resting the towel over his shoulders.

"Adrik!" he snapped.

Chuckling, I patted what I could dry without being inappropriate and then handed him the towel to finish the rest. Once done, I crouched and held out the boxers for him to step into. By the time we made it back to his bedroom, where there were clean sheets applied to the bed, West was breathing heavier.

"Do you need pain medication?" I asked, helping him to sit on the side of his bed.

I worried when he did not reply for a few moments. Finally, he shook his head and looked up at me. "Maybe soon, but… could you help me out to the living room to sit at the table for a while?"

Hope resurfaced inside me. "Of course."

CHAPTER SIXTEEN
WEST

$\mathcal{Y}$ou are the biggest liar," Kylo complained with a groan. He threw his cards to the table while Saint grinned evilly.

"I damn agree. Show me your pockets," Death said, crossing his arms over his chest and leaning back on the seat.

Saint stood with a smirk and shook out his arms. "Nothin' up my sleeves." His hands slid into his jeans pockets and pulled out his wallet, a packet of lube, which had my face flushing as well as Kylo's, and some coins. "Nothin' in my pockets." His hand went to the button on his jeans. "I can strip to show you everythin' if you still don't believe I'm just skilled and not cheatin'?"

"We do not need to see everything," Adrik said crisply and went as far as covering my eyes. Chuckles sounded around the room.

Smiling, I tugged his hand away and pushed my cards into

the middle of the table. "Saint, you can't win five times in a row and not be cheating," I put in.

"I can. By bein' just that awesome."

Kylo snorted.

Saint draped an arm around his shoulders. "Lover boy, you can't deny my skills."

"Are we still talking about cards? Because if we aren't, I don't need to know anything more about my brother," Lucas said. Wreck walked up behind him from the kitchen and placed a cocktail in front of him. He leaned in and kissed Lucas's cheek. It brought a soft smile to my friend's face.

A hand squeezed mine, and I looked down. I still held Adrik's from when I took it from my eyes. Heat hit my cheeks, and I quickly let go. His hand turned over and rested on my thigh. My heart took notice and increased its speed. I gripped the back of the chair in my hands since I sat on it backward, ensuring my back didn't rest against anything.

Adrik had been clear he was interested in me. Only his attention rattled my nerves. A lot.

What I wanted for him was not me. He could do so much better than a scarred college dropout who had many issues that needed to be worked through. Yet, I couldn't bring myself to set him up with someone, to shove him in the arms of someone else. I was being selfish and keeping him close because he was my calm.

I had been to see a psychiatrist a couple of times in the last ten days, and my friends were right—it was good to talk to someone. I had a feeling the sessions could help, but it was too soon to tell. I still held so much anger and fear inside me.

However, ever since my breakdown in the shower, I hadn't lashed out at anyone.

My anger wasn't meant for them but for the people who raised me. The people who did this to me. But they were dead. Without being told, I knew what the men around me would have done. They would have taken care of the threat. In one way, I was grateful; in another, I wanted those who'd hurt me so badly to rot a long life in jail, but now they couldn't.

There was still so much to work through. Like my friends, and even my psychiatrist, had said, it would take time.

Some days I couldn't help the despair creeping in. It ate at me in many ways, but most of all, it told me I wasn't good enough for the people around me.

I was filth.

Dirty.

Horrible.

"Moya lyubov'?" was whispered beside me.

My heart skipped a beat, and I blinked out of my daze. I glanced at Adrik. His smirk had my pulse racing. It was like he knew my mind had drifted into that dark place, and he was there to drag me out. Either with sweet words or a touch.

I offered him a small, grateful smile and nodded. I ignored my nerves enough to place my hand over his to hold on to.

"I'm okay," I told him quietly as the others bantered around us.

"I know this."

My smile grew. Of course Adrik knew. The man was

confident he would bring me out from the darkness. I liked that about him. I liked a lot of things about him.

I quickly looked down at the table when my eyes got watery.

Adrik was my rock. My strength.

He was my knight in shining armor.

He was a light in my darkness.

It was impossible not to fall for him. Even though it had only been a short amount of time, my feelings for Adrik were strong.

It scared me. I feared he would see I wasn't worth it, but that was my own insecurity. I was blessed Adrik saw something in me I couldn't yet find myself.

Sniffing, I discreetly wiped my eyes on my shoulders. My back twinged from the move and brought a grimace to my face. Clearing my throat, I picked up my one and only beer. "Here's to Lucas and how he's going to kick ass in the exams."

Lucas's eyes shone over at me. His smile wobbled a little. He wished I was taking the exams with him. But as I'd explained to him, I wasn't in the right frame of mind, and I wasn't sure I ever would be. I wouldn't give up my dream of becoming someone who would help people, but I needed time to think about what I really wanted.

Death had said he was ready when I was to take me on in the security office where I would have a job watching surveillance cameras. It paid as well as Polished did. I hadn't told Adrik as yet. It was only a couple of days ago that Death mentioned the job when he wasn't around. But really, anyone could guess I would never go back to Polished, even when I'd healed, because of my scars.

I wasn't at the stage where I was supposed to be proud to wear them because it apparently showed how strong I was. To me, they were ugly and reminded me of a night I wanted to erase from my head. It reminded me of parents who tortured their son because they believed he sinned.

I couldn't wait for the day those marks on my skin wouldn't disgust me, anger me, upset me. Until then, I just had to keep going. Even at my darkest times when I thought about ending my life, I knew I wouldn't, because... well, I wanted to live.

I wanted to love.

That special kind of love that Lucas and Kylo had.

That special kind of love where only one person was made for you.

And I couldn't help but think that Adrik might be that one for me.

He'd stuck with me when I was cruel and mean. He'd stuck by my side since that day, and it wasn't him wanting to fix me. He was patiently waiting, willing to be a part of this fucked-up situation and to be there for me when I finally found myself. Found peace.

He cared before the attack.

He wanted me when I'd wanted him, right from the start.

Why else would a man have someone watched? It wasn't that he didn't trust me. He was watching over me.

I had completely fallen for Adrik Mikhaillova, and knowing this, I reverted into a young schoolboy with his first crush. I fumbled and bumbled around him, stuffing up my words and actions.

It was lucky I knew Adrik found me amusing… well, if his lip twitches and smirks were anything to go by.

I wasn't sure I'd ever understand what Adrik saw in me, but it must be something special, because he slept at my side every night. He read or would talk when I wasn't in the mood, even when I'd been a prick and ignored him.

Though, it was always hard to ignore Adrik.

My psychiatrist always got this small smile on his lips when I spoke of Adrik, especially when I explained how stubborn and annoying he was because he wouldn't leave me alone. I was sure he found everything Adrik did cute.

Like when I told the psychiatrist I had been in a mood and wanted to be left alone, and Adrik didn't listen because he'd heard my stomach growling and thought it was a good idea to have a picnic in my bed where he got crumbs everywhere.

Then again, after I'd discussed it and now thought of it, I did find it cute also.

Adrik got my heart racing, palms sweating, blood pumping, and my dick thickening.

Still, I wasn't ready for the next move. I still had doubts and fears to work through.

A knock sounded on the front door. Dimitri, who sat in the living room with Country, Tech, State, and his woman, Courtney, called, "I will get it."

Wreck glared down at Adrik for some reason. Of course, Adrik reciprocated it with a sinister smirk. I didn't understand their hate for one another, but Lucas told me not to worry about it. Kylo had also mentioned it was just their way of measuring who had the biggest dick. I wasn't sure who had won, since they ignored each other most of the time.

"Adrik," Dimitri said, coming into the dining room.

"Da?"

"It is your parents."

Oh shit.

My stomach dropped to my feet, and I gulped. Adrik had told me about them. Said they'd stuck around to meet me before they went back to Russia, but I wasn't sure if I was ready to see them, because they knew what had happened.

Paling, I stood. "I'm… um, going for a walk."

Shit, the front door was through the living room. My bedroom was through the living room.

"Now?" Lucas said, shock evident in his tone.

"Ah, sure." I nodded. At least I could go out the back door.

"But your back," Lucas tried.

"It's better." And it was. The ache was always there, but from what Lucas told me, the burn, that fucking burn, had scabbed over. The cuts were also healing, so I didn't see why a walk would be bad.

"West," Adrik started.

I couldn't look at him. Shame had my stomach twisting. "Sorry," I whispered.

"Son?"

I jolted from the voice behind me and then froze.

Fuck my life. I should have kept an eye on the doorway behind me instead of my exit.

Adrik stood. "Father, it is good to see you."

"You also."

"Lucas, we have that thing to do," Wreck said.

I pulled my wide gaze up as my pulse sped up. *Don't you dare leave me,* I sent telepathically, but of course, I didn't have that power.

"Right, yes, that thing." Lucas nodded. "Excuse us."

"Adrik" came a female Russian voice.

"Mama." I saw Adrik embrace a shorter woman out the corner of my eyes.

"Saint."

"Yeah, we've also got something to get to." Saint smiled.

"Good to see you both, Mr. and Mrs. Mikhaillova," Kylo added before he too deserted me.

"I ain't got a good lie, so I'm just gonna say I'm outta here to give you all some privacy," Death said as he stood.

My mouth unlocked in time to reach for my last escape. "Death, I have to talk to you about that job."

Death snorted. "Kid, don't even try it. We can talk later." He gave me a two-finger salute and left.

"West," Mrs. Mikhaillova said softly.

I was out of luck. I had to face them, since running from the room wasn't a cool thing to do. Not if I wanted to keep Adrik in my life. Sweat formed on my hands and the back of my neck from nerves.

My face bright red, I turned to see an older version of Adrik and a woman who looked like a fairy with beautiful blonde hair and blue eyes.

"West, this is my father, Nicholai, and my mother, Annika. Papa, Mama, this is West."

Tears pooled in Annika's eyes, causing my bottom lip to tremble and emotions to rise. I cleared my throat, opened my mouth, but only a sound came out. I pressed my shaky fingers to my lips. My eyes widened again.

Nicholai's jaw clenched. I worried I'd failed him or Adrik for a moment until he stepped forward, cupped the back of my neck, and pressed his forehead against mine. I slammed my eyes closed as they welled and a sob caught in my throat.

"I am sorry for what you have been through."

Reaching up, I gripped his wrist and held on.

"I am sorry for the pain you have. But you are here. You have the heart of our son, so I know your life will get better. You will have a cherished life wanting for nothing. A life well deserved to you."

My throat thickened. He didn't know me. He only knew his son cared for me.

Nicholai pulled back. My eyes fluttered and tears dropped. Nicholai smiled and gently patted my shoulder. "It is good to meet you, West."

I nodded, unable to speak, worried I'd cry like a little boy.

Nicholai moved aside, and Annika stepped up. I flinched when her hands cupped my face. Shivers ghosted over me, and more tears pooled at her soft expression. But I couldn't stop the fear from rising. My breath became ragged. After all, it was a woman who did the damage to me.

"Nyet, Mama," Adrik tried.

She didn't listen. "It is hard knowing others have heard what happened. You are a brave, handsome man who was mistreated by people who should only love."

My blood froze.

I didn't want to hear this.

I didn't want to deal.

I shook my head, lifting my hands. I pressed them against her arms and shook my head again.

"Mama," Adrik growled.

She ignored him. "It was they who were born wrong. Their minds were corrupted. Not yours." A noise escaped through my lips. My body vibrated with the need to get away from her words. But her hands slid to my shoulders, her grip tightening a little.

"Mama, *dolvol'no*," Adrik clipped, and I felt him move closer.

"Adrik," his father warned.

Annika said softly, "No mother should hurt their child."

"Don't," I begged.

"Dolvol'no," Adrik yelled. I heard a shuffle, but I couldn't look away from Annika.

One of her hands cupped the side of my neck. "She was a monster. She was evil. Know that if you were my son, I would love you with every breath I take."

"Please," I choked, tears blinding me as they filled and dropped.

"I would love you, West, because you are none of those things she said to you."

"Then why?" I screamed. "Why did she do it to me?" I dropped to my knees, and Annika came with me, cradling my head as I bent over, letting the agony take over. "Why would she do it?"

"Because she was never blessed with love. She did not understand what an amazing child she created. She was lost in her own created world of lies and hatred. She was lost, West. But you are not. You are here with us. You are loved. I may not know you, but I already know I will love you, my boy. I will."

"It's not fair," I uttered through cries.

"You are right. It is not," Annika said softly. "But all we can do is keep moving, keep going, and pray nothing like that happens again." I nodded and held her tightly as I cried once more over the injustice of all that happened to me.

"Enough now," Adrik said, his tone harsh. "You are in America, not Russia. Not everyone likes tough love," he snarled.

I didn't want him upset with his parents. Even though I felt as if a truck had hit me, I knew I needed this.

Lifting up, I scrubbed at my face and sucked in a shuddering breath. The agony seemed easier to breathe through. I glanced up at Adrik, who stood with his arms crossed, glaring at his parents.

"Adrik," I said. His eyes flashed down to me. I held my hand up to him. "H-Help me up." His hand slid into mine, and he pulled me to my feet while Nicholai assisted Annika. I rested my side into Adrik's front and reached out for Annika's hand. "I'll freshen up, but please stay for dinner?"

I could feel Adrik's gaze on me, but I kept my attention on his parents. Both smiled. Nicholai even seemed proud. He stood straighter and his smile grew.

"We would love that," Annika replied.

"I'll just need a moment," I told them, and with Adrik's hand in mine, I made my way to the bathroom. Only once we were in the abandoned living room, Adrik pulled me to a stop. Facing him, I looked up into his eyes.

"West, I never knew they were coming or what they would say."

My heart leaped to my throat, but I pushed on my nerves and rested a hand to his chest. "I know. I… I didn't expect that type of reaction." I licked my suddenly dry lips and glanced to the side in thought before meeting Adrik's intense gaze as he studied my face. "I believe it was good for me, though."

His lips thinned. "Still, it should not have happened. Not from them." His jaw clenched. Reaching up, I traced a thumb over his jaw.

"Don't be angry with them."

"They upset you. I will be angry with them."

I smiled. "Not too angry then. I'd still like to have dinner and get to know them." And by the end of the night, maybe my emotions would settle enough to actually get to know them. "Besides." I shrugged. "It'll be my first chance to have dinner with the Russian mafia."

He laughed unexpectedly even as his eyes widened with shock before he quickly clamped his lips shut. But he chuckled once more. Leaning in, he kissed my jaw. "You are something else, moya lyubov'."

Moya lyubov'. My stomach did a summersault and then tried the high beam. The other day I had Google translate those words and found out exactly what they meant.

My love.

All this time he had been calling me his love.

I dropped my head to his chest and damn swooned. "I'm a good something else, right?"

"Always."

"Okay."

Moya lyubov'.

I would never get bored of hearing those words slip from his lips. Not when he said it as though I was someone he wanted to worship.

Yeah, I couldn't explain why he thought I was it for him, but I was starting to allow him to believe it because I wouldn't want a day to go by without seeing Adrik in it.

*L*ater that night, I lay in bed beside Adrik and watched him read from a new series we'd started. "Adrik," I interrupted.

"Da?" He pressed a finger to the spot he was up to and looked down at me lying on my stomach. I hadn't yet managed to rest on my back; it was still too tender.

"Your parents are amazing."

He snorted, glancing to the door. "They are okay." He was still frustrated they'd upset me. Even throughout dinner he was curt with them, which they ignored.

"You're lucky to have them."

His jaw clenched. "Most days."

Reaching out, I rested my fingers against his hip. "Don't be too mad, Adrik. Does it seem like I regret the choice they made? How they spoke to me?"

"Not yet."

"What about I promise nothing they said or did will cause

me any… damage?" Because I honestly didn't think their actions would come back and bite me on the butt. They were tough, but in that moment, it was what I needed, and I didn't even know that.

"You cannot promise such a thing."

"I can and I will."

His lips thinned. "We will see."

All I could show him was how it didn't negatively affect me like he thought. It would take time for him to believe it, but he would see. For now, a change of subject was needed. "Has there been any further development from the church?"

His nostrils flared. Shit, it probably wasn't the best choice of topics.

"Nyet," he clipped.

I blinked. My mind went to one point only. "So, it was only my… only them who did this to their child."

Adrik moved. He put the book on the bedside table and slid down the bed to lie on his side facing me. "West," he whispered.

I closed my eyes for a beat and shrugged, which twinged my back a little. Opening my eyes, I gave Adrik a sad smile. "I guess it's good news."

His fingers grazed my chin, neck and then rested against my jaw. My stomach somersaulted.

"Tell me about this job with Death." It looked like it was his turn to change the subject.

I lifted my hand to wrap around his wrist. "In his security firm. In the surveillance rooms."

He tapped his fingers against my jaw. "And this is something you want?"

"It's a good job for now and pays well."

"Are you done with Polished?"

I glanced away from his intense gaze, needing a moment to catch my breath. "I doubt the way I am would be good for clients."

He gently pinched my chin, bringing my eyes back to his. "As long as you are speaking of what you have been through and not the scars you hold."

"Adrik…."

"West, did I not tell you about when I first saw you? That I had to walk from you in that moment because you had made my lonely heart beat in a way it had never before."

"Adrik," I whispered, closing my eyes.

"You are beautiful. Even with your scars, moya lyubov'. One day you will believe me."

My love.

Those words shot an extra pulse to my chest.

"You undo me, Adrik."

"In a good way?"

Heat hit my face; Adrik chuckled and ran a finger over the globe of my cheek. I closed my eyes. "Yes."

"I am glad, West, because you do the same to me. Ever since the first day."

Meeting his gaze, I asked, "Would you eat ten chocolate muffins if I asked?"

Humor hit his face. He laughed and leaned in to kiss my chin. "For you, yes. I would risk my perfect physique for you."

I groaned and tightened my hold on his wrist. "You remember that?"

"I do. I liked hearing you say it."

"Your confidence is big enough. I shouldn't have said anything."

"But the way you blushed and bumbled around after was charming."

"Stop," I moaned, flushing.

"West?"

I glanced back at him. "Yeah?"

"In the next week, would you go to dinner with me?"

It sounded a lot like a date.

Did he mean a date?

He probably did since we already slept in the same bed for the past few weeks. It would be normal for two people to go on a date after that.

After he gave another gentle pinch to my chin, I slammed my eyes back onto his. "Do you mean… as in… we go on a date?"

His smile was wicked. "Da, moya lyubov'. A date."

"Oh…." My body warmed at the thought of walking into a place with Adrik at my side so people knew he was with me. He was mine. And boy, did I want him to be mine in every way.

"West?"

"Yes!" I blurted a little loudly. Adrik gave a low chuckle.

"Good, moya lyubov'. I will make arrangements."

"Okay," I uttered.

His gaze drifted down to my lips.

Yes. Kiss me.

A kiss was okay, right? We liked each other. We slept beside each other. We touched each other. All right, maybe Adrik did reach for me more than I did, but I never would regret any caress from him. I loved them in fact—the way he would reach out to me or kiss my jaw, cheek, temple, and forehead.

I wanted one on my lips, though.

So much.

But he didn't. Instead, he pulled his gaze away and rolled to his back. "Are you ready for sleep, or would you like me to read more?"

I wanted him to face me again and kiss me. My heart and body agreed with my mind.

But how did I make it happen?

Could I ask?

Just the thought of saying the words had my stomach dropping to my feet.

Could I push through my nerves and just say it? Would he want to kiss me?

I licked my dry lips and opened my mouth to ask. Only the words wouldn't come out. I snapped my mouth closed and cursed myself.

I was a chicken.

Adrik would want a kiss. He was here and had been with me every night. He liked *me* and would want a kiss. I didn't have to be so scared over the words.

"West?" He turned his head my way.

"Huh?"

His smile was warm, probably as warm as my face. He placed his hand behind his head, and his T-shirt rode up and exposed skin.

I gulped.

"Would you like to sleep or for me to read more?" he asked again.

"Adrik."

"Da?"

I cleared my throat and followed his body up to meet his gaze. "Would you…." I made a noise in the back of my throat.

Adrik rolled to his side, up on one elbow, and looked down at me. Heat seared his gaze. "Would I what, moya lyubov'?"

I scraped my bottom lip with my top teeth and made a move to sit up. Ignoring the tight pull to my back, I faced him, sitting cross-legged on the bed. I picked at the sheet as I stared at it.

Adrik's hand rested on mine. He still lay on his side, and it was my turn to look down at him. "I am guessing you do not wish to sleep, since you are sitting."

"Yes." I nodded.

"Moya lyubov', what is it you are after then?"

Hoo-boy, here we go.

My heart threatened to beat out of my chest, but I managed to get the words out. "Kiss me." My eyes widened. "I mean… you don't have to. I know this is new, and you've been sleeping here. I don't know—" I squeaked out the last part as Adrik sat swiftly and leaned in with his nose close to mine.

"I would give you anything, West."

His lips brushed against mine once, twice. My ears rang from freaking butterflies bursting to life inside me.

"More?" he asked, his voice thick with... desire?

"Yes," I whispered.

A hand slid to my neck, to the back of my head, threading through my hair where Adrik gripped. I gasped, and Adrik took the opportunity to press his mouth against mine, to gently glide his tongue over mine.

Reaching out, I held onto his T-shirt and shifted closer to deepen the kiss. Our tongues danced, our breaths mingled, our hands caressed.

It was more than I thought it would be.

It was amazing.

Adrik broke the kiss. Both of our breaths were ragged. "Christ, West," Adrik muttered.

I wanted more. No, I needed more. I tugged on his T-shirt. "Can we?"

He groaned in the back of his throat, moved back, and removed his T-shirt, throwing it to the floor. I caught a glimpse of something on his back, and before he could turn my way, I grabbed his arm.

"What's on your back?"

"A tattoo."

Oh, heavens above. The man just got hotter.

I pressed a finger to my bottom lip and pinched at it. "Um, can I see?"

Adrik studied me with a smirk. "You like tattoos?"

"Uh-huh." I nodded. "Yep." It was a weakness of mine.

Adrik turned away from me, placed his feet on the floor

beside the bed, and rested his hands on the mattress on each side of him to let me have my eyeful.

Hot damn. It was all I could think over and over. I'd never seen anything so ferocious and yet stunning in my life. A dragon's head covered most of his back. A beautiful, scary dragon. It was perfect for Adrik.

I rested my palm against his back. He shivered. I bit my bottom lip and ran a hand over his smooth, warm skin, as if I petted the dragon.

"It's gorgeous," I told him.

"West," he clipped.

"Hmm?"

"I will need to kiss you now."

"Okay," I uttered.

He turned so fast I gasped. His hand cupped my cheek, and his lips were back on mine. I moaned into the tangle of tongues, the brushing of lips. Reaching out, I placed my hands against his chest. His naked chest. Hard planes of muscle greeted my palms. Slowly, I ran them down the dips and ridges of his stomach and felt it move under my hands. My arm brushed against something before a hand gripped my wrist and brought it up just as the kiss broke off to a sweet caress of the lips against each other.

Adrik pulled back and kissed the back of my hand. He shifted around until he was on his back with his arm out my way.

"Come here, moya lyubov'. On your stomach, rest your head on my chest."

Smiling, I felt the blush rise, suddenly shy even after the

kissing. I slid down the bed and curled an arm over his stomach, resting my head to his chest.

This was nice.

Sweet.

I let out a breath and opened my eyes to see the hardness in Adrik's sleep pants. It matched my own. A fresh new blush hit my body all over. Adrik pulled the blanket over us, covering a sight I wanted to stare at for some time more, but I didn't say anything.

What we'd done was enough.

I could wait. Even if my dick was crying over the travesty. I wanted our first time to be exactly like it was tonight.

Perfect.

CHAPTER EIGHTEEN
ADRIK

We used to sleep on our separate sides of the bed—until the night we shared a kiss. Now, I woke with West sleeping in my arms, and I could not be any happier. It had been a week since that night, and I knew with the amount of healing West had done, it was creeping closer to the time I would have to get back to work.

It was not something I wanted to do, but if we were to keep this going between us, I wanted to make sure it grew into something strong. I needed to give us both time to get back into our normal everyday lives. Besides, West was to start his new job at the end of next week. I tensed at the thought of him leaving my side or the safety of the house, but I reminded myself he would be surrounded by men I trusted.

West nuzzled into me. His head tipped back, and he lazily blinked up at me. My heart caught on a beat when he smiled.

"Morning."

"Good morning, moya lyubov'." I dipped and kissed his

forehead. I was free to kiss him when it came over me to do so. Each time I enjoyed the cute smile he gave me, along with the blush.

Mostly when I first did it in front of people. West had been sitting in the living room when I got back after having to step out for a moment. I couldn't even remember what for, but all I could think about was getting back to West. I had walked through the front door to see him surrounded by Kylo, Lucas, and Lucas's parents. I greeted them but kept my gaze on West as I approached. I had planted my hands on the armrests and leaned in to take his lips in a hot kiss.

"Oh my" had come from Mrs. Storey.

I rested my forehead against his and said, "Moya lyubov'."

"Um... hi."

I had grinned and stood. "Would anyone like a coffee?"

After taking their orders, I had moved off but heard. "Herb, why don't you greet me like that?"

"Fuck me, now I won't hear the end of this."

West was getting used to me kissing him in front of people, since it seemed I could not help myself when it came to him. Now he expected it when I was around, and every night since the first. Though, it was getting harder and harder keeping my hands to myself. Especially since we both became aroused from being alone and having each other's mouths.

"Do you have to leave today?"

"Da. I have a few things that need my attention." He nodded against me. "I was wondering if you would like to go to dinner tonight?"

He buried his face into my chest and nodded.

"Words, moya lyubov'. I need them."

He kissed my chest, and my dick perked up more than it already was from having him in my arms.

"Yeah, dinner out sounds good."

"Excellent. I will organize a place and pick you up at six."

"Sounds good."

"Would you be interested in staying at my home after?"

He paused after a little yip sounded from his lips. I pinched his chin and gently dragged his head up to see his cheeks burning for me.

"Yes?" I asked.

"Da," he replied.

"Good. Pack a bag then. Now kiss me so I can get ready for the day."

Of course, when he did, I did not leave the room for another half an hour.

WEST

"I feel like a giddy gay teen on his first date," I confessed as I sat on my bed, gripping the sweater I held.

Kylo snorted. "Shit, I would as well if an ex-mafia guy, who was hot and totally fuckin' devoted to me, was on his way to pick me up for a night of sexy time." He grinned and quickly added, "Don't tell Saint I called your guy hot."

Lucas and I laughed. "I won't if you don't call him hot in that appreciative tone again."

"Well lookee here. Someone's possessive," Kylo teased.

"It's good to see," Lucas said. He took the sweater from my hands, folded it, and placed it in my bag. "I bet you never thought you and Adrik would be where you are."

I shook my head. "Not in a million years. It might sound like my head's in the clouds, but I never thought I could be this lucky."

"He's as crazy for you as you are for him. Anyone can see it," Lucas said.

I hummed under my breath, my body warming. That I believed. The man kissed me every chance he got, no matter who was around—even in front of Dimitri and his parents, who'd been over for lunch before they departed early the next day to go back to Russia.

"What are you wearing to dinner?" Kylo asked.

I glanced down at my jeans and T-shirt. "This."

Lucas and Kylo shared a look.

"What?" I demanded.

"You can keep the jeans, but maybe try a shirt. I'm sure Adrik will take you to a nice place," Lucas said.

Groaning, I slapped my forehead. "Crap. I should have thought of that. I don't have a nice shirt. At least I don't think I do." I strode to my walk-in closet and flung shirt after shirt across the room. None of them felt right. "No, no, no," I repeated. I groaned. "I don't have anything."

A chuckling Kylo rested his hands on my shoulders. "Relax. He'll like you in anythin'. Go out and finish packin'. I'll find somethin'."

"Okay." I nodded, relaxing a little.

Lucas helped me with the rest and slid in a packet of condoms. I froze, my gaze rising to his. Lucas smiled. "Just in case."

My face burned.

Lucas shifted closer, his hand dropping to my arm. "West… um, it's natural to want something from Adrik."

My goose bumps extended down my neck. "Lucas," I moaned, definitely embarrassed.

"Your back is healed enough for a little playtime."

"Oh my God. Do not call it playtime."

"Sexy time?" Kylo suggested, walking back into the room and holding a plain white shirt. "White is always good."

I waved him off. "White, sure. And no to sexy time. I am not talking about my… my time with Adrik. I don't even know if he'll want to touch me—" I clamped my mouth shut, not meaning to voice one of my fears.

"West," Lucas whispered as he shook his head.

Kylo rested his cane against the bed. "West, I get why you would think that. Hell, I felt incomplete with my injuries, but from what I've seen, you'll have a hard time keeping his hands off you."

"He's right," Lucas agreed.

I knew it, deep down I did, but I couldn't stop the worry about a naked night with Adrik. I wasn't even sure I was ready for more.

"Besides, it's not like you have to jump his bones right away. There's other things you can do." Kylo wiggled his eyebrows up and down. Both Lucas and I blushed. Kylo laughed in response.

All right, I could do this. I could get over my anxiety of Adrik being anywhere near my back. He liked me. He stayed at my side. He wanted me, and I wanted him just as much. I wouldn't miss out on a chance to deepen what Adrik and I had, especially over my injuries that Adrik had already seen.

Nodding, I rubbed at my chest over my beating heart. "You're both right."

Lucas grinned. "Aren't we always?"

"I wouldn't go that far," I told him. I replaced my T-shirt with the crisp white shirt. "This good?" I asked, holding my arms out for inspection. Lucas gave me two thumbs-up.

"If I didn't have a man, I'd jump you," Kylo said.

"Then thank fuck you have me," Saint said from the doorway, glaring at Kylo. Lucas and I jolted, while Kylo just turned to his man and grinned.

"That's true. I see no other besides you."

Saint grunted. "Keep it that way. You ready to head out?"

Kylo shook his head. "I have to stay to see West off on his first date with Adrik."

"Ah, no you don't," I said. There could be a chance I'd make a fool out of myself somehow, and the fewer people who saw it, the better.

Kylo grinned. "Yes, I do."

"I'd really prefer if you all weren't here," I said, and picked up my bag from the bed. I started for the door as a grinning Saint stepped back to let me through.

"Now we definitely have to stay," Saint said.

Shit.

Just as we rounded the door, there was a knock. My

stomach swooshed. I glanced there to already see Wreck opening the door. I got a glimpse of Adrik before Wreck shut the door in his face again.

"Wade," Lucas scolded.

Wreck sighed and opened the door again. "In," he ordered.

I quickly moved that way. "That's okay. We can just go." Lord above, when my gaze landed on Adrik and I got a good look at him, my breath hitched, and I stumbled.

Fuck my fears. I would have a part of him tonight.

The suit he wore molded to his body nicely.

Chuckles sounded around me as Wreck stood in front of my exit. "Not yet," he clipped over his shoulder at me.

"Wait, what?"

"What time will you have West home?" Wreck demanded harshly. Adrik just glared back at him.

"Dear God," Lucas groaned and moved around me to place his hands on Wreck's waist. "Wade, West is staying at Adrik's tonight."

"I didn't agree with this," Wreck stated.

"See, I knew staying long enough would be entertaining," Kylo said. Saint agreed with a chuckle.

Oh, heavens above. Wreck acted like... like he was my father.

My throat thickened.

"I don't like it," Wreck grumbled.

"Thankfully, West is old enough to make up his own mind," Lucas said.

"Enough," Adrik bit out. "I have lived here for a few weeks—"

"And I didn't like that either," Wreck sneered.

Adrik snarled, "West is coming. I will protect him. Your small brain knows that, at least."

Wreck actually growled under his breath. Kylo and Saint just laughed some more.

"All right," I called. I shifted around Lucas and Wreck and stared up at the big man. "I appreciate your concern. I really do, but I'm going out with Adrik."

Wreck's jaw clenched. "Fine. But call if you need us." He glanced over my shoulder. "I'd be happy to kick his ass if he does something you don't like."

"Oh my God, please stop," I begged, and before I lost my nerve, I swept in and hugged Wreck quickly before facing Adrik. I didn't want to see Wreck's shocked gaze. I smiled softly. "Ready?"

"Da, moya lyubov'." His hand shot out and took my bag for me before it came out once more for my hand.

"Have a good night," Lucas called.

"I am sure we will," Adrik replied, his tone tighter than usual as he stared down at me. Heat hit my cheeks, and when we started down the path, I tripped on nothing. It was lucky Adrik was there to catch me. Laughter started behind us, and I sent the middle finger over my shoulder.

"Dimitri's coming?"

"Da. As he puts it, he is my head of security; I do not move without him knowing. He will watch over us."

A shiver swept over my body. "Are you expecting trouble?"

We stopped at the passenger side to Adrik's car. I waved to Dimitri in his own vehicle, which he returned. I glanced back to the house to see the others had gone back inside. But then Adrik's hand cupped my cheek. I faced him, tipping my head back in time to have his mouth on mine.

"There will be no trouble. Dimitri is just a... what do you say, worrywart?"

I grinned. "That's it."

"I am businessman. I have people wanting attention. The security keeps them at bay."

"Okay."

"You trust me to take care of you?"

Of course I did. Lucas had told me how he saw Adrik lost with rage on my behalf. I'd asked for the details the other day, and Lucas mentioned how he'd never heard such an animalistic roar come from someone before, but he did and then witnessed Adrik advance on that man and snap his neck. All in a matter of seconds. Apparently, he'd been wracked with fury on my behalf.

I rested my hand on his chest. "I trust you with everything, Adrik."

His eyes darkened right before he claimed my mouth in a wild, searing kiss.

I looked forward to seeing where the night would take us.

West looked from the restaurant back to me. His gaze ran over me, and he bit his bottom lip. He had not leaned all the way back in the seat, since it agitated his back, but right then, he had once again tilted all the way forward to study the restaurant I had picked to eat at.

"Are you sure I'm dressed all right for this place?" he asked once more.

"Da, you look good." My voice came out a little lower than usual, agreeing wholeheartedly with my words. West looked good enough to eat.

"Adrik, I don't know."

Smiling, I opened my door and told him before I climbed out, "You will be fine."

"What was the holdup?" Dimitri asked where he waited in the cooling breeze after a warm day.

I walked around the car and opened West's door. "West is worried he does not look good for the restaurant."

Dimitri chuckled. "It just means he is trying to impress you."

West gasped as he exited. "I am not!"

"See, he is very defensive. Means he cares."

"Shut up," West grumbled and stalked toward the front entrance. Both Dimitri and I laughed.

I had never felt this light before. My chest expanded with the warmth I felt for the man still muttering to himself. It had something to do with Russian men.

I quickened my pace to slip in front of him and open the door. West's glare at me made me grin.

"Your one has fire inside him."

"Da, he does."

"I'm going to kick the both of you in a second," West said, pausing just inside the door for us.

"Please do not. You might hurt yourself, and then Adrik will blame me and make me bleed."

West's eyes widened as he looked from Dimitri to me, noticing Dimitri's serious face. I did not defend myself. What Dimitri said was true.

"You wouldn't," West hissed.

I took his hand and led him toward the front counter. "I would."

West shook his head, snorting. "You two are full of it." Yet, I could see the uncertainty in his eyes.

"Do not fear. Adrik would feel bad afterward," Dimitri taunted some more.

"He is wrong," I said.

"Hello, how can I help you?" the waitress asked.

"I have two bookings. A table for one and a table for two under the name Hail."

"Yes, sir, I see it right here."

"You're not joining us?" West asked Dimitri as the waitress grabbed some menus.

"There is no way I would intrude on your first date. I am here to enjoy a meal and keep an eye out."

West blushed. Dimitri smirked and looked at me. "He is cute."

"I agree, but that will be the last time you comment on it."

Dimitri chuckled. "Yes, sir."

"Right this way, gentlemen." The waitress smiled sultrily at us. Obviously, she did not hear our conversation or chose not to, or she would have known neither West nor I were interested.

I retook West's hand. I would never get bored of seeing the heat hitting his cheeks. The waitress showed Dimitri his table first and took his drink order before leading us to ours. It was not far from Dimitri's, but enough to have some privacy.

"Can I get you any drinks for now?" She leaned in and placed my menu before me and turned to do the same for West, only she lingered a little longer and smiled warmer.

"Water," I clipped.

"Um, I'll have a Coke, please." West gave me big eyes, not noticing how she looked at him. I did not like it. Not when she licked her lips either.

She pressed her hand to West's arm. "Coming right up."

"Touch him again and I will—"

"Thanks!" West shouted, startling her. When her smile dropped away at my glare, satisfaction filled me. She quickly walked away.

"Adrik—"

"She had no right to touch you."

He smiled softly. "No, she didn't, but I think she's got the message now."

I grunted and picked up my menu.

"Besides, the only person who is free to touch me is you."

I glanced up to see West hide his face behind his own menu and knew color would be staining his cheeks.

Smiling, I said, "Good to know, moya lyubov'."

"Anyway," West drew out, "what looks good to you?"

"You," I stated.

He coughed out a breath and glanced around, his blush deepening. "Adrik," he scolded.

"I do not care who hears, West. I hid my life long enough. I will no more, not when it comes to you."

Despite him biting his bottom lip, his smile was evident. "I… um, like that you don't have to hide."

"It was stupid of me to begin with since my parents are supportive. However, Russia is a very different place to here. It also helps I am no longer in the mafia."

The waitress made an alarmed noise in the back of her throat. I had already heard her coming, another reason I mentioned the mafia. It was not something I would usually, since I had cut all ties to it, but it should not matter with one insignificant woman.

"Though I am still very connected to it," I said and stared

up at her. She gulped and placed our drinks on the table with shaky hands. West groaned and knocked the menu into his forehead a couple of times.

"A-Are you ready to order?" she asked with a curtsy.

"Nyet, give us more time."

"Right away." She curtsied again and quickly disappeared.

"I'm afraid you've scared her."

"Good. It lets people know not to mess with us."

He opened his mouth, then closed it.

I thinned my lips, concerned. "Do you not like the way I deal with things?"

He quickly shook his head and reached across the table to lay his hand on mine. "You be you and do whatever you want, because I'll like you no matter." He smiled and picked up the menu again. "I might act shocked, but in the end, it doesn't faze me."

My chest expanded once more over his words. No one had taken me for who I was. Until West.

It was his fault I was going to keep him.

"All right, I'm going to have the chicken and pumpkin risotto." He nodded and placed his menu down on the table. "You?"

"Steak," I replied, pushing my menu away from me. "Moya lyubov'?"

His smile was soft. "Yeah?" He picked up his glass.

"Where do you see yourself in five years?"

The glass paused against his lips before he regained his thoughts and took a sip. He cleared his throat and placed the glass back on the table. "Five years?"

I nodded. "Da."

I sensed movement beside us and glanced there. The waitress was hesitant to approach. Good. "We are ready," I told her.

She shifted closer. "Great, what would you both like?"

After we ordered, she quickly skuttled off like a scared mouse. It was never my intention to intimidate her. I would have let slide the smiles, but when she touched West, my body burned with anger.

West cleared his throat. "Are you looking at going back to work soon?"

I raised a brow. "Do not think I have forgotten you did not answer my question."

He bit his bottom lip and shrugged. "I just need time to think about it and answer."

"I will give you this time."

He laughed. "Gosh, you are too kind."

I smirked. "I know, and to answer your question, I will be back to work when you start at the security company."

He played with his bottom lip, pinching it and driving me crazy. "Well, I guess I have held you up long enough."

I flashed my eyes up to his and dipped my brows, confused. "But you have not. I attended to work during the day still."

He smiled. "No, I mean, that we'll be in different areas for work, so we won't get to see each other as much as we do now."

"I will have Death move his company close to my office."

West snorted, laughed, and shook his head at me. "You're unbelievable. You can't do that."

But I could. I would buy Death an office space if I had to. I rested my elbows on the table, my chin on one hand. "Do you not wish to see me in the evenings?"

His eyes flared. "No, that's not what I meant."

"So you like the sleeping arrangements?"

His cheeks pinked. "I do. Do you? I mean, if you think it's too soon, I understand."

"It is not I who is thinking of sleeping away from one another."

"You don't think this is all too soon then?"

"Do you?" I countered.

He shrugged, then shook his head. "I just worry that we'll burn out."

I sat back. "It is good then that we work apart during the day. But I would not like to sleep without you at my side, West. If this is something you do not wish to happen, please tell me."

I doubted I would sleep if I did not have him close.

Time had been wasted when I'd fought my feelings for him to begin with, and I would regret it always. I did not want to waste any more time without West in my life.

"I... um..." His blush burned brighter. "I'd like to keep things as they are."

"By sleeping at my side?"

"Yes," he whispered.

"Good. We will talk about you moving in with me later."

"Adrik, no… I can't…." His mouth snapped shut. His brows dipped, and he stared down at his drink.

"It is something we are already doing, only at Lucas and Wreck's house. I could do without seeing Wreck every night."

"I was just thinking the same thing—not about Wreck, which I really don't understand why you two can't just get along. But I was thinking that we practically live with one another already."

"Exactly. If you agree now, I will call Dimitri to send men to Lucas's to collect your things."

He chuckled, shaking his head again. "How about I stay at your place this weekend and see how things go? We can decide on Monday."

"If you wish." I already knew that come Monday, West would be moving in with me. But if he needed those days to get his mind around it, he had them.

"I'm going to slip to the restroom before our dinner gets here." He stood and went to walk by, until I took hold of his wrist.

I tipped my head back and met his gaze. I held it until he grinned in understanding. He bent and briefly kissed me on the lips. It was enough.

While he was gone, I pulled out my phone to make a call.

"You do know I am not far away" was how Dimitri answered.

"Da. I need you to do something. Contact Death to see if he would move his business closer to my offices. If it is not something he wishes to do, look at selling the condo, and I will move closer to West. We will buy some clubs to run in that area."

Dimitri whistled. "I never thought I would see the day that my friend would be completely taken by someone and willing to alter their life in ways."

"Just do it."

"Yes, sir." I could hear the smile in his voice.

Moving one way or another would make the commute shorter for either of us. That meant I would have more time with him.

By the time West dropped into his seat again, our meals had been delivered. I waited for a reaction from his food, but instead, he looked guilty about something. He rubbed his hands up and down his forearms and looked everywhere but at me.

"What?" I demanded.

His eyes clashed with mine. "What, what?"

"Something has happened in the time you went to the restroom and here. What was it?" Did I have to hunt someone? Hurt someone? Kill someone? I ground my teeth together and glanced around while I waited for an answer.

"Okay, so it was nothing really."

"West," I bit out.

"The waitress caught me in the hall and asked if I needed help to get away from you."

"What?" I snarled.

"I told her she was a fool and that I didn't. Don't stress about it. I didn't want to tell you because of the way you would react, but I'm no good at keeping things in."

I stood. West moved quickly to shift in front of me. His hands landed on my chest. "No. This will not ruin our first date. Who cares what she thinks? I set her straight, so it's fine. Please, for me, sit back down and enjoy our time here."

I stared down at him and tried to calm my thoughts. It irritated me that she had the balls to approach him after everything. Still, for West, I would be reasonable for once.

Only West must have read something different from my expression because he blurted, "I know what *myela voush* means."

An abrupt laugh dropped from my mouth. "What?"

His face heated. I loved how he blushed so easily. "You know, what you call me."

"Moya lyubov'?"

"Yes, that."

Grinning, I gestured to the seat, letting him think his distraction had worked. "Please, we will eat, and you can tell me how you have heard of it."

"Oh… um, okay." He nodded and started to move back to the table. Before he could escape, I took his wrist in mine and quickly planted a kiss on his neck. His pulse in his wrist increased against my fingers. I smiled inwardly before I released him and took my seat.

I placed the napkin over my lap while I waited for West to say more. When he stayed silent, I looked over at him. He was already shoveling food into his mouth.

"This is good. So good."

I shook my head. "Moya lyubov', you got away with the

change of subject before by saying you had to think about it. I will need to know how you found out about your name."

He set his fork down, cleared his throat, and after a sip of his drink, he said, "Google Translate."

I drew my brows up, surprised. "And it understood your pronunciation?"

"Did I mince it up?"

"A little. But I found it cute."

He scraped his bottom lip with his top teeth in thought.

"What, moya lyubov'?" I asked.

His soft gaze rose. "You've called me that since… then."

"Da."

"Why? It means, 'my love,' right? Why would you call me that back then?"

"Because I knew I could not live my life without you in it."

His eyes closed, and he drew in a shuddering breath. A small smile touched his lips. "Okay," he whispered. Opening his eyes, he nodded toward my food. "You'd better eat before it gets cold."

There it was: acceptance. Elation filled me that West acknowledged my truth. I had been worried he would not care for my words, but having had him take on what I said and move on, told me I did not need to hope he was mine.

He already was.

*D*inner was amazing. On top of the company and comfortable conversation, it had been the best risotto I'd ever tried. When I told Adrik, he had a taste and informed me that his was better. On the drive to the condo, I pushed my nerves down enough to mention, "You know I can't cook. I can bake but not cook."

Would he worry about that?

"Da, I remember those muffins. I will teach you if you would like?"

Warmth spread through my body. "I'd love that."

He took a hand off the steering wheel to take mine and rest it on his thigh. "Good. I have many dishes to teach you."

"But just remember it'll be your fault if I ruin a delicious dish."

"With you saying delicious, it reminded me of the times you ate my meals and moaned like you had just come in your pants."

I gasped. "Adrik," I snapped. I couldn't believe he'd just said that.

"It is true. I had never been so hard before."

I pulled my hand free and pushed at his shoulder. I loved his teasing, but my face burned in mortification. I hadn't realized I'd moaned like *that*. "Oh my God. I can't believe you said that."

"What? The truth?"

"Well… even still, it's embarrassing I moaned like that, *and* it was the first time I met you."

He retook my hand. "I will forever be grateful I went through the business to gain company, or I never would have met you."

I squeezed his hand. "I'm glad too, but… why did you? You're a hot guy with an accent. You could have found anyone."

"I wanted it on my terms and where you would expect nothing from me but my company. At the time, I wasn't interested in finding a partner. I went on dates, but they wanted things I didn't want to give—more of my time or money."

"You did go on dates?" Jealousy reared its ugly head in my gut.

Adrik glanced at me and grinned. "Da, but it had been a while, long before you came along. It is good to know you become jealous as I would."

Rolling my eyes, I mumbled, "Whatever." Of course he chuckled. I understood where Adrik was coming from. He was lonely in a way where he craved company but didn't want to have to put on the charm for a date. He was mostly himself right from the start, and I loved knowing that. The first night had been a test to see if we connected, to ensure I wasn't dazzled with his condo and such. With the rest of our time together, he let himself show in more ways than he had the first.

I was just happy I had the real Adrik.

We drove into the underground parking area, and Adrik stopped close to the elevator. I got out and went to grab my bag from the back seat, but Adrik already had the back door open, taking it. Smiling at his chivalrous behavior, I walked around the car, and we made our way to the elevator.

"Isn't there usually people around?"

"Dimitri called ahead and got rid of them."

"Why, and where is Dimitri?"

"Because I wanted to do this." He slid his card through the keypad and then faced me. Dropping my bag to the ground, he cupped my face and kissed me. I stumbled forward, bracing my hands on his hard chest when he deepened the kiss. He pulled away, and I whimpered. His smirk was cocky. "My men fear me. If they see the sap I have become around you, they would think me soft."

"You are soft," I teased.

"Only with you. Actually, with Dimitri being up there with them, they are probably watching this on the cameras. I just wanted you alone down here."

I stilled for a second before I pushed Adrik's face away and looked around for the cameras. When I spotted one, I ducked behind the car.

"May I ask what you are doing?" Adrik questioned, the humor evident in his tone.

"Shit, I don't freaking know. My head jumped to cameras and being caught. I panicked."

Adrik's phone rang. "Da? He panicked when I mentioned cameras." I could hear Dimitri's loud roar of laughter from where I crouched. Standing, I shot a glare and the middle finger to the camera. Thankfully, the doors to the elevators dinged open. I swiftly made my way inside.

Adrik ended the call, picked up my bag, and chuckled his way over.

"I looked like an idiot." Turning into Adrik, I pressed my face into his chest. "Your men will think I'm foolish."

He snorted. "I doubt that. I'm sure you will charm them."

"I know, I'll bake them something."

"You will not. They are my baked goods."

His rough tone sent a shiver over my body. "Okay," I got out before Adrik was kissing me again. I heard the bag drop as I wound my arms around his neck, and Adrik circled my waist with his.

The doors opened too quickly. Both panting heavily, we parted. I wanted more of that, but while we were naked.

"Bed?" I asked softly. I stepped into Adrik's condo and looked over my shoulder, catching Adrik adjusting himself in his pants.

"We do not have to do anything— Fuck," he clipped when I pulled my shirt over my head. Panic caught me for a moment, but all I had to remind myself was that it was Adrik. The man I loved. The man who wanted me as I was. Scars and all. I sucked in a shuddering breath and watched his chest rise and fall rapidly. "Are you sure?"

My heartbeat was erratic, and I felt like I was going to burp with the amount of rolling my stomach did. But I wanted him. I needed to show him. I popped the button to my jeans, loving the way Adrik's eyes darkened.

"Your back—"

"Is healing, and as Kylo said, there are other things we could do... or I could be on top?" I shrugged, turned, and started for where I thought Adrik's bedroom would be. I didn't hear his footsteps behind me, but I kept going, or I would lose my nerve, and I thought I acted pretty cool... and thinking that made me sound like a dickhead.

Adrik did want me, right?

Was I supposed to ask him?

Did he actually want to do something with me?

No. I couldn't let my mind think otherwise. The man had asked me to move in with him. I still couldn't believe his offer. Thinking about us together permanently had my stomach fluttering and a smile blooming.

I wasn't sure why I asked for the weekend to think about moving in when I already knew the answer. I couldn't imagine a night without seeing him.

I pushed through the door at the end of the hall and smiled. A king-size bed lay opposite the door. To the right were two doors; one would be a bathroom, the other a closet. To the left were windows that led to another balcony. The light from the moon was enough for me to see the bedsheets were dark, as were the walls and the bedside tables. Adrik certainly loved dark colors.

I looked in on the large bathroom, complete with a jacuzzi in the corner. The closet held all his expensive suits, shoes, other clothes, a million belts, and watches.

After I was done inspecting, I made my way back into the bedroom to find Adrik leaning against the doorway. My bag at his feet.

Heavens, he was gorgeous.

I swallowed thickly, my nerves rising once again.

He straightened and glared over at me. "I had to wait for the elevator to come back up since you distracted me, and I forgot your bag."

Laughing, I said, "You look a little flushed there, Adrik."

"You are standing in my room half-naked, moya lyubov'."

"And that makes you hot?"

His smirk was wicked as he removed his jacket and dropped it to the floor. I gulped, my pulse raced, and my dick throbbed when he slowly undid the buttons of his dark shirt. He pulled it free from his body and dropped it as well.

He hummed under his breath, his eyes lighting with humor. "You are flushed also, moya lyubov'."

"No," I squeaked. I cleared my throat. "I'm fine."

"Are you sure?"

Nope. "Yep." I nodded. My eyes widened when he undid the button and zipper of his pants. He kicked off his shoes, and I did the same, but my gaze stayed glued to Adrik. His socks were next. I started on mine, tripped, and stumbled forward, drawing a chuckle out of him.

"I'm good," I told him. I stood on the toes of my other sock and slipped my foot from it.

Adrik's grin died when I hooked my thumbs into my jeans and pushed them down my body, which left me in my boxers. My dick tented them.

"Christ," he clipped.

I shot him a cocky smirk, but it faded when Adrik dragged not only his pants but underwear down his legs. His cock bounced free—hard and ready for my attention. And boy did I want to give him all my attention. I could imagine dropping to my knees and taking him in my mouth, sucking and licking him. Heck, I would even pet him because he had such a stunning long, thick dick.

"Moya lyubov'," Adrik growled.

I blinked, looking up to meet his gaze. "Huh?"

"Take your boxers off and sit on the bed. I have a need to feed you my cock from the way you are looking at it."

Nodding, I pushed my boxers down, tripped over them on the way to the bed, and sat on the side of it. My dick throbbed, and my heart galloped as Adrik stalked my way.

He stopped right in front of me. "I was going to ask again if you are sure, but I can see how eager you are for this between us." He cupped the side of my face. His thumb pressed into my mouth. "I like that, West. A fucking lot."

I shivered. "Good," I said, my voice husky.

His hand slid to the back of my neck when I rested my hands on his thighs. My gaze traveled to his leaking cock. He gripped my hair and gently tugged my head toward him. I opened my mouth and licked at the tip, tasting, savoring his flavor.

"Khristos," he uttered.

I wrapped my lips around the tip, and Adrik slid his dick all the way in, drawing out a deep grunted moan from him. He pumped a few more times until he dropped his hand and stepped back. "I am not ready to come." He dropped to his knees, and in the next beat, his mouth was on my cock. I let out a shocked but pleased cry. He licked, sucked, and teased, drawing out my precum with his hand.

My balls thought it was ready to unload, but it wasn't.

"Shit, hold up," I panted. Adrik pulled back, a cocky smirk on his wet red lips. I patted his shoulder. "Yes, yes, you're as good as me in driving each other crazy."

He chuckled and stood, holding out his hand. I took it, and he pulled me to my feet. Smiling, I wrapped my arms around his shoulders and his looped around my waist.

"Do you want to go further, or we could just keep doing what we are?"

"Further, please."

His eyes lit. He took my mouth in a hard, deep kiss, and his hands slid down to my ass. He tugged me forward, and we rubbed our cocks against each other.

I needed him.

Like now.

"Please," I begged against his lips.

"Turn around, moya lyubov'." When I did, he pressed his cock against my ass and reached around to take hold of my aching dick. "I have been tested, West."

I nodded, finding it hard to catch my breath because his hand on me ran up and down my length. "Same."

"Bare?"

"Yes."

"Fuck," he groaned, kissing my neck. "I love you, Moya lyubov'. I need you to know this."

My heart burst with damn rainbows. Reaching back, I rested my hand on his thigh. "Love you, Adrik. And I'm pretty sure it happened the first day I saw you."

"Da, West. For me as well." He ground his cock into me and kissed my neck again. I arched to give him better access. "Let me prep you, moya lyubov'."

"On the bed," I told him.

Adrik shifted to the bedside table, opened the drawer, and took out a bottle of lube, which he placed on the sheets. He climbed onto the bed first, lying on his back. He put his hands behind his head, content to watch me with, honest to God, smoldering eyes.

Leisurely, I lifted my knees onto the bed and scooted closer before I kicked one over his hips and rested my ass back onto the top of his thighs. With a cheeky smile, I placed my hands on his lower stomach. His cock twitched, wanting attention like my own dick did. Only I didn't give it to them. Instead, I ran my hands slowly up to his ribs, his chest, and then back down his arms. I glided them over again and again on his warm flesh.

"You're gorgeous," I whispered.

"Nyet, Moya lyubov'. That is you."

Grinning, I shook my head. "We'll have to agree to

disagree on that."

"Da." He smirked, but it was replaced with a question, "I can touch, da?"

"Baby, you can do anything you want."

He groaned. "Do not tell me such things. I want everything from you."

"You already have my heart, Adrik. There's not much else to give."

"Your body, your soul. All of you."

"Then take it, baby. It's all yours."

He gripped my upper arm and pulled me down to claim my mouth. I let out a little yip but moaned as soon as I got his tongue in my mouth. I loved kissing him and could do it all day and night. It got me hotter.

I ground down over him, and he nipped at my bottom lip before deepening the kiss again.

Adrik slipped his hands down, jerking me up so he could cup my ass. I didn't know when, but he'd already slicked his fingers, and when he ran them over my hole, I shuddered. He circled around the edge and slipped in slightly when he started kissing me down my neck. I panted and moaned.

He nipped at my throat, but I wanted his teeth in me. I wanted him to suck, bite, and mark. "More," I demanded. "Teeth and fingers."

Adrik groaned harshly and bit down, sucking my skin into his mouth, and he slid another finger inside me, both gliding over my prostate.

"Fuck," I cried. "Feels good, baby, so good." I held on as he played with my body, using his fingers and mouth like it was his own instrument. "Need you," I pleaded. Already I was too close, and I wanted to finish with him inside me.

Gently, Adrik pushed on my shoulders, and I sat up.

"Take me inside you, moya lyubov'," he ordered roughly, lust driving his tone.

He handed me the lube. I squirted some on my hand and pushed up on my knees, reached between us, and wrapped my hand around his rock-hard dick, rubbing lube all over him. His grip on my hips hardened. A noise in the back of his throat, half growl and groan, followed.

I held him at my entrance, met his gaze, and slowly slid him inside me. It burned for a moment. Adrik clenched his teeth and sat up enough to kiss me tenderly, his attention distracting me from the sting. I removed my hand and lowered myself even more, breathing heavily against his lips.

"Fuck, moya lyubov'. You undo me."

I hummed under my breath and finished lowering until he was all the way in. I rocked and gasped when his cock rubbed against my prostate.

"Adrik, so good," I whispered.

"Da, moya lyubov'. You feel good."

I rocked on him again and again, lost in the feel of him inside me. Enjoying the sensation it sent right to my balls, I gasped.

Opening my eyes, which I hadn't realized I'd closed, I looked down at my man. *Mine.* He watched me take what I wanted, but I needed to give him what we both desired.

Resting my hands on his chest, I inched up off him to near losing the tip and sank back down. Both of us let out a hard breath. I did it over and over as sweat formed over my body and Adrik's.

"Adrik," I moaned.

"Close, moya lyubov'."

Knowing it had me slamming up and down on him. I wanted to feel the burn of him tomorrow and the next day. Hell, I wanted him inside me tomorrow and the next.

I couldn't stop. I reached for that climax, and it burst through me. I yelled as my cum squirted out over Adrik's stomach and chest, marking him.

"Yes, West. Fuck, fuck," Adrik groaned, holding me in place as he dug his heels into the bed and fucked up inside me, losing himself, emptying himself.

I draped myself over his chest, where he kissed my neck, cheeks, and forehead. "You will never get rid of me," he told me drowsily.

My heart gave off an extra heavy beat. My body was satiated in a way I hadn't felt before. This was more than I ever expected it to be. Being with Adrik was perfect. I smiled big and pressed my lips into his shoulder. "Good." Because I never wanted to lose him. He was made for me, and I couldn't wait to see what our future held.

Embedded in West's ass was fucking heaven. I would never get bored of taking him. And from the moans and whimpers, he enjoyed it as much as I did. The way his ass squeezed around my cock as I took him on all fours was torturous in the best way.

"Adrik, baby," West whispered on a moan. He was close.

I ran my hands over his back. He was used to my touch, used to my attention all over his body, but especially his back. I dropped a kiss to the scar of the cross and slid my hands up to under his arms, where I tugged him up, moving with him. His arm curled around my neck, which arched for me so I could bite down, groaning over his skin.

"Yes," he hissed.

I pounded into his ass but held his upper body tightly. "Moya lyubov', the way your ass clamps around me drives me crazy. I am close."

"God, baby. So am I."

I glided my hand from his chest down to his cock and gripped. His cry of release had me clamping my teeth onto his skin again. I knew he loved it when I did so. His arm tightened around my neck, and he kept coming over the sheets on the bed.

"Fuck," I clipped. I groaned loudly with a grunt. West was like a vise on my dick, so too soon, I was releasing into his tight hole, filling him with my cum.

West hummed, running a hand through my hair before tilting his head around to have my mouth on his. I wanted to stay buried inside him until I was hard again so I could fuck him once more. However, we did not have time.

Moya lyubov' would need attention like he did after every time we were together. I slipped out of him, dropped to the bed, and tugged him down on top of me.

"Adrik, we'll get cum all over us."

"You think I care, moya lyubov'? I do not."

West laughed. "Neither do I. Okay, five minutes of this, and we'll go for a shower."

"Do we have to go?"

He slapped my chest. "Of course we do."

A knock sounded on our door. "Are you two done? You have a reception to get to." I could hear the amusement in Dimitri's voice.

"We are not coming," I called.

"We are," West shouted and rolled off me. I growled under my breath and tried to grab him, but he was quicker. He stood beside the bed, utterly naked and fucking gorgeous, as he smirked down at me.

"You have to since it's your own, Adrik," Dimitri said. "I'll meet you down there in five."

"Twenty," I said.

"Ten," West countered.

We heard Dimitri sigh. "Half an hour, and that is it. People are waiting on you two."

Standing, I curled an arm around West's waist and kissed my marks on his neck. "You have made me the happiest man today."

West shook his head as I lifted mine, and he cupped my cheeks. "You're wrong. You made me the happiest, husband."

"I love hearing that coming from you."

"Good, because you'll hear it all the time. Even when I'm pissed at you for not picking up your clothes."

I snorted. "It is not I who does not pick up after themselves."

He grinned. "I'm just trying to keep you on your toes. Now, let's go shower, thank everyone for coming to our wedding, and get back up here as soon as we can."

"I like the way you think, moya lyubov'."

My father had told me earlier that he was proud of the man I had become, but I would not have been who I was without West standing at my side.

WEST

"Look at him. He can't take his eyes off you, and you just got plowed," Kylo said.

"What the hell?" I snapped, hitting him on the arm.

Lucas laughed. "No need to be embarrassed about it, West. Not when he's your husband. Besides, you came back down with fresh marks on you."

I groaned and glared at my husband, which he laughed at. Of course, the sound brought a smile to my face. Not only seeing him laugh but knowing he was mine. Forever.

"I still can't believe he asked Death to move the business his way," Lucas commented.

When he'd told me, I couldn't believe it either. I thought he'd been joking when he told me. Then he decided since Death wouldn't move, he would. I told him he didn't have to change his life for me, but, as I had learned, when Adrik decided something, he made sure to follow through. Nothing seemed to be an obstacle for him. He moved into the top condo in a new development and made sure we lived together a few days later.

Two years we'd been together.

Two amazing years. Even when we fought, the makeup sex made up for it.

"He gets what he wants in the end, and the clubs he bought are thriving. We're looking at taking a month away for our honeymoon."

"Just you, Adrik, and Dimitri?" Kylo smiled.

I shrugged. "Probably. Though, knowing Adrik, he'll take a couple of other men."

"He's just as protective as Wreck." Lucas laughed.

"Thank fuck those two finally got over their hatred for one another," Kylo said.

"I know," I groaned. "It only took a year, and they still like to give each other shit."

"It's their way of showing they care," Lucas said as he shifted on his feet. "I have something to tell you both," Lucas said.

"You're pregnant," Kylo teased with a chuckle.

"Well, no, but—"

I gasped. "Oh my God, you found a surrogate?"

Lucas beamed. "We did."

"Fuck, man, that's awesome news." Kylo hugged Lucas to him.

When they parted, I pulled Lucas into me. "I'm so happy for you."

"Thank you," he whispered.

As Kylo and Lucas spoke of names depending on if it was a boy or a girl, I glanced at the rings on Lucas's and Kylo's fingers. Lucas had married first, a year ago. Both Kylo and I were his best men. Then Lucas and I were Kylo's when he married Saint six months ago.

I never thought I would get past what had happened, but I did, and a lot of that was because of the people in my life. My own special family.

I still worked at the security company and was happy there. It might have been a waste not to go back and pursue a medical career, but I didn't let it bother me. I was happy. Giddy happy. Each day I woke up beside Adrik, I thanked my lucky stars for bringing him into my life.

Who would have thought a job as an escort could lead me to the man of my dreams, but it had, and I would always be grateful.

ACKNOWLEDGMENTS

Thank you to my readers for loving West and wanting his story. It was hard to write because of what West had to deal with. No one should go through what West did, and if anyone in the world doesn't feel safe or is scared, please reach out to people you know who will care and love you no matter who you love!

A massive thank-you will always go to Jay at Covers by Juan. I absolutely love his designs and look forward to working with him every time.

Becky at Hot Tree Editing, you know how much I adore you. Liv and Donna, you ladies rock!

To my beta ladies, Lindsey, Amanda Berry, Amanda Evans, Miranda, Nikki, Darlene, and Annissia for deciphering my words before it even hits the editors.

ALSO BY LILA ROSE

Polished P&P Series

Wreck Me Forever (Lucas and Wreck)

Never a Saint (Kylo and Saint)

Hawks MC: Ballarat Charter

Holding Out (Free)

(standalone related to the Hawks MC: *Outplayed*)

Climbing Out

Finding Out (novella)

Black Out

No Way Out

Coming Out (m/m novella)

(standalone related to the Hawks MC: *Out to Find Freedom*)

Hawks MC: Caroline Springs Charter

The Secret's Out

Hiding Out

Down and Out

Living Without

Walkout (novella)

Hear Me Out (m/m)

Break Out (novella)

Fallout

Standalones related to the Hawks MC

Out of the Blue

Out Gamed (novella)

Romantic Comedies

Making Changes

Making Sense

Fumbled Love

Trinity Love Series

Left to Chance (m/m/f novel)

Love of Liberty (m/m/f novella)

Titles under L. Rose

The Hidden Kingdom Trilogy

(Reverse Harem)

A Torn Paige

A Lost Paige

A Final Paige